Midsummer Night

Also by Uwe Timm

Midsummer Night

Uwe Timm

Translated by Peter Tegel

A NEW DIRECTIONS BOOK

The publisher extends thanks to Rebecca Penn and Claudia
Steinberg, each of whom provided helpful suggestions in regard
to the translation.

Manufactured in the United States of America
New Directions Books are printed on acid-free paper
First published in 1986 as *Johannisnacht* by Kiepenheuer & Witsch,
    Cologne
First published clothbound by New Directions in 1998
Published simultaneously in Canada by Penguin Books Canada
    Limited

Library of Congress Cataloging-in-Publication Data
Timm, Uwe, 1940–
    [Johannisnacht. English]
    Midsummer night / Uwe Timm : translated by Peter Tegel.
        p.   cm.
    ISBN 0-8112-1372-2
    I. Tegel, Peter.   II Title.
PT2682.I39J6413   1998
833'.914—dc21   97-42140
                                                  CIP

New Directions Books are published for James Laughlin
by New Directions Publishing Corporation
80 Eighth Avenue, New York 10011

Contents

Swift as a shadow, short as any dream,
Brief as the lightning in the collied night,
That, in a splee, unfolds both heaven and earth,
And, ere a man hath power to say "Behold!",
The jaws of darkness do devour it up:
So quick bright things come to confusion.

William Shakespeare, *Midsummer Night's Dream*

Midsummer Night

Napoleon's camp bed

STRICTLY SPEAKING, THIS STORY BEGINS WITH my not being able to find a beginning. I sat at my desk and pondered, I roamed through the city. I took up smoking again, cigars, hoping that, swathed in smoke, the right, the absolutely essential beginning to a story would occur to me. It didn't help, I just couldn't get into writing—that first, all-decisive sentence simply wouldn't come. At night I stood at the window and watched a woman in the house opposite who'd recently moved in and and who received her male visitors in the brightly lit apartment. I also tried writing about that: a man who watches a woman and assumes she knows he's watching her. But after a few pages I quit. I went to a North Sea resort and roamed the length of the beach in an April storm, my head filled with the roaring of the surf, the screech of gulls, and the complaints of the hotel owner whose only guest I was. After four days I fled back to my desk. I'd bought myself a chess program and was playing on my laptop through Kasparov's games from the last world championship. In the afternoon of the fourth day—I still hadn't got beyond the opening moves of the first game—the phone rang. A magazine editor asked me if I would be interested in writing something about potatoes: the Peru-Prussia connection. Potatoes and the German mentality. And of course personal potato preferences. Recipes. Fried potato affairs. He laughed. "You're interested in stories about everyday things, aren't you. Eleven to twelve pages, you can spread it out."

I said I was deep in other work at the moment and so didn't have the time. Actually, I had just been mulling over a chess variation with the strange name of "The Tree." After the call I tried to get back to concentrating on the game, but instead I began to think about my uncle Heinz. Because this uncle could taste the different kinds of potato, even when they'd already been boiled or fried. When he was dying, after days of not saying a word, he said something strange: Red Tree. Nobody knew what he might have meant. My mother supposed it was a kind of potato. In the family, at least by my father, my uncle was considered lazy, a shirker and a failure who spent his life smoking on a couch. That is also the clearest image I have of him in my own memory: Uncle Heinz lying on a sofa in the kitchen, his head pillowed by a cushion on the armrest. He's smoking. He could blow the most wonderful smoke rings. If I asked him to, he'd exhale a chain of three rings. One Sunday shortly after the war, he and aunt Hilde were

invited for a visit. My father had been foraging for potatoes at the farmer's. And now my mother was frying
potatoes. The table was laid with what remained of the
silver that hadn't yet been bartered off with the farmers
for provisions. We all sat and waited. There was a smell
of fried onions, even of bacon, because my mother had
greased the pan with bacon rind. It was a feast, Mrs.
Scholle and Mrs. Söhrensen, with whom we were billeted at the time, were at the table too. Uncle Heinz was
the first to be served a few fried potatoes. He chewed
carefully, tasting the way people taste wine do, a gentle
movement of a slightly open mouth, an inward listening. He hesitated, slowly shook his head, thoughtful,
really brooding, so two more slices were put on his
plate. Again the careful chewing. My father asked impatiently: "So?"

My uncle swallowed, deliberated, and then after
hesitating a moment: "It's the Fürstenkrone!" "Bravo!"
my father cried, and we all clapped. At last we could
eat, those weren't just fried potatoes, they were fried
Fürstenkrone! They tasted wonderfully. But what did
they taste of? When I asked my uncle he just said:
"Well, there aren't words for that."

Red Tree. Strange, what goes through a dying
man's head just before he loses consciousness.

Perhaps, I thought, it's not a bad idea to accept a
commission for once, if only to create a little space for
myself and this story that didn't want to have a begin-

ning. I could certainly use the money and also Kasparov's opening moves had lost some of their attraction; so I phoned the editorial office and asked if the potato story had already been given to someone else.

"No."

"Good," I said, "I'll write the article. I'm interested in the connection between tasting and telling. After all, both have to do with the tongue." The editor stopped short, but then named the fee, and then because, surprised at the amount, I was silent for a moment and he misinterpreted my hesitation, he added that I could also claim traveling expenses for research.

"Good," I said.

That same day I ordered five books from the State Library and began reading: about the history, the nutritional value of the potato, about cultivation methods and recipes. I was lost in ever more remote areas: potatoes in Ireland, Indonesia, and on the island of Tristan da Cunha. I enjoyed frittering away time on the nomenclature—Grüblingsbaum, Tartuffel, Erdapfel, Grumbeere—and finally realized it would make more sense to first talk with someone who had an overview of potato research, a historian or a nutritionist.

In the evening I phoned my friend Kubin who had moved from Hamburg to Berlin after the Reunification and there—after four years of working for the privatization firm Treuhand—had set himself up as an independent management consultant. Not only was Kubin a good cook; in his spare time he was also writing a book about traditional Italian cuisine.

"Just a second, I'm about to burn some food here," he said and then a moment later, yes, he even knew somebody who'd thoroughly researched the potato. "Here in Berlin. I'll get you the address."

The next day I flew to Berlin in order to do some very ordinary research.

Kubin was waiting by the elevator and as we briefly embraced I noticed he'd put on weight. He looked tired, grey, unhealthy. "Come in," he said, "good to see you. But this time strictly in confidence—I don't want to turn up in a novel again."

He showed me through the apartment. Four spacious rooms. One room was empty except for three massive stone eggs, polished, two of marble, one of black granite, as if a roc had laid a clutch of eggs here and might at any moment come in through the slightly open window.

"The Berlin room," he said, "serves as a passageway, it leads to the bedroom."

"Nice and quiet, faces the yard."

"It does," he said, "but still, I had such insomnia in this asshole city, I once even dozed off during a meeting I was holding. It was just that I couldn't sleep in bed at night. Now I do sleep, you could blast cannons off right next to me, I won't wake. No more dreams either. At any rate, I wake up in the morning without remembering any dreams. I grieve deeply in a deep sleep. And you know why it is, this mindless, even immoral sleep? It's strictly because of the bed. I bought it two years ago. Come, I'll show you."

He led me into the bedroom: a bare room with nothing in it but a cupboard and a bed. The bed was a simple camp bed.

"What do you think of it? It's an exact replica of Napoleon's camp bed. You can see the original in the Paris Military Museum, but sixty centimeters shorter. He slept on it on all his campaigns. Short, but deep, as we know. It was the only way he could cope with the tremendous strain. The bed's absolutely perfect, it's hard but because of the springs—how can I put it—it carries you. Like the waterbed Angela and I bought ourselves for our wedding. Who doesn't have the desire to walk over water or sleep on water? But then all that duckweed."

"Duckweed?"

"Originally the bed was flesh colored, but after only a month it turned green, algae, we were told, the bed suddenly smelled like a cave, and two months later like a carp pond. We carried it secretly to a woods, organic compost, as it were, and bought ourselves a Japanese bed, Samurai style in fact, king-size. There would have been room for a concubine as well. It stayed behind, like the marriage, in Hamburg."

He went ahead of me into the kitchen, in which there was nothing apart from a sideboard, a table, a refrigerator, a gas stove, none of those fancy copper pots on shelves, no crocheted potholders by Hopi Indians on the walls. Only a print signed by Andy Warhol: the Campbell's soup can. Kubin had already set the table for two: the silverware, the plates, the glasses from the twenties, designed by a Bauhaus celebrity. He took the spaghetti and let it drop into the boiling water like mikado sticks, fanning out artistically.

"I even wondered whether I shouldn't have a number of these camp beds made. But then I gave up the idea. There's just no market for them in Germany. The conservatives are too provincial, and, unlike their comrades in France, the left-wingers aren't drawn to military things."

A lamp hung down from the kitchen ceiling, the shade in white glass, on it black figures like cut-outs. Elves and children with nets chasing a woman with butterfly wings. "Yes," said Kubin, who had seen me looking, "I bought the lamp in Vienna at the Naschmarkt. It works because of the wings, as you can see."

"A fairy?"

"Perhaps, or even perhaps a Nike. Whatever it is, they are after her wings. Have you ever thought how the French turned a catastrophic defeat into victory through sheer stone mass? Just take a look at the Arc de Triomphe. The names of all the battles are engraved in the arch. Defeats as well as victories, so this gigantic stone arch even vaults over catastrophes like Leipzig and Moscow. Looking at the Arc de Triomphe no one would think that Napoleon had lost decisive battles, or even the war. That's aesthetics, you see, one sees things differently, that's what it's about." Kubin poured olive oil into a pan, warmed it, added a cup of pesto, said "fresh pignoli, that's important." He took a paper bag from a shelf—"hold out your hand"—and poured a few pine nuts into my hand. "Why, of all things, are you interested in this proletarian among the vegetables?"

"That's just it."

Kubin carefully took out a bottle of red wine from the wine rack, uncorked it, smelled the cork, poured me a glass, said: "Now, guess."

I tasted, "Hard to tell," I said, "Italian, Montepulciano? But from the Abruzzi! My guess: '93, a good year."

"I'll be damned," he said.

"No," I said as he looked astounded, "I read the label."

Kubin took a sip, carefully smacked his lips, and said: "Emidio Pepe," and then he stirred the pesto in the hot pan. "Potatoes, not me, I belong to the noodle faction."

"I once fell in love with a potato."

Kubin asked furtively: "What kind?"

"A student. At a student costume party. This girl was dancing, dancing wildly, but as a new potato, a delicate light brown, a bit rosy like a belladonna lily. Her favorite meal: baked potato skins with cottage cheese and chives. That being the reason for the delicate pale coloring. She had a few green freckles on her nose. 'Freckles are the tiny windows in the skin,' I said, 'to absorb more sun in the grey German Niflheim. That's how you prevent rickets.' She said, 'I hope I've got enough. I've only got freckles on my nose.'"

"And," Kubin asked, "was that true?"

"Don't know. After all, she was wearing a round wire frame, covered in a reddish-brown material. She pulled me—I'd come as Don Quixote—onto the dance floor. It was an indescribable night, the only student party that I don't remember as boring. Probably has to do with the fact that I couldn't get near her. All because of that beautiful new-potato covering."

"And then?"

"She disappeared in the early hours, like Cinderella. I never saw her again. Sometimes when I look at the delicate skin of a new potato her image takes me by surprise, and I gobble down the potato in a surge of memory."

"Good," said Kubin, "that's a reason for writing about them."

"Do you know what Red Tree means?"

"Red beech?"

"No, I don't think so, I think it's probably a kind of potato. They were the last words of an uncle who could taste the various kinds, like you the vineyards."

"I'd have liked him. Ask this potato expert," he said. "I met him more than a year ago at a party. An agricultural scientist, he was in the GDR Academy, then he was removed. One of some thirty thousand who hung around in dilapidated institutes and busied themselves with research on something unusual like the history of the 18th-century Sun Writers or who drew up the grammar of ancient Uzbek or counted the stones in the ruins of Thebes. When they weren't busy writing reports about each other. His name was Rogler. A quiet sort with a bearable Saxony dialect that had amalgamated with Berlinerish." Kubin drank some red wine, he slurped, smacked his lips, said: "Aah. You only noticed the Saxony dialect when he started talking about potatoes. Then he let it rip, a real Pentecostal miracle: potatoes, nutritional value, morphology, spread, God knows what, there was no stopping him."

"Exactly the man I'm looking for."

Kubin had me taste the pesto. "Well? Quite simple but really good," and he smacked his lips again. "You can keep your potatoes."

"Have you got this man's address?"

"No. But you can ask Rosenow, an academic col-

league of his, also let go. I deal with him, he earns himself a few marks as an advisor to a real estate firm. I've
written down his telephone number for you." He
pointed to the table where a note was lying by the napkin, went to the sideboard, took a colander, drained the
spaghetti in it, and then, with a wooden ladle, mixed it
in the bowl with the pesto.

"Red Tree, doesn't exactly sound like a potato."

"They have the strangest names."

"What did your uncle die of?"

"Lung cancer. He smoked at least forty cigarettes a
day; he was still smoking in the hospital, spitting blood,
but kept on smoking secretly in the bathroom. And
then he died and his last words were: Red Tree."

"Ask this Rogler," Kubin said and took more
spaghetti. "You can say what you like, but the Italians
know why at most they offer potatoes only as a side
dish. Unlike tomatoes. Of course they mustn't be these
Dutch hothouse monsters. I buy my tomatoes from an
Italian, he grows them here in Berlin on an allotment,
he gets his manure from the police riding school."

For the rest of the evening Kubin complained about
Berlin and the Berliners, especially about how they
were always trying to be witty and ready with an answer, in other words the Berlin gab, it got on his nerves.
And he got to talking about Angela, his former wife,
who had just married for the third time. This time to an
American botanist who specialized in arctic lichen and

was now looking for a job in Berlin, which, as you can imagine, isn't that easy, as in the East as well as the West there are any number of lichen specialists looking for jobs. "I saw him once, he's like a flying squirrel, you know, those animals that leap from tree to tree and steer with their tails." Kubin talked, and some spaghetti dribbled from his mouth. He slurped the Italian red wine, wiped the greasy rim of the glass with a napkin, and said, "I'm curious to know whether, with her IUD, she'll be able to avoid getting pregnant with this botanist. A real marsupial mouse."

"Marsupial mouse?"

Kubin took a hefty sip, gazed lost in thought at his plate, then twirled the last of the spaghetti around his fork. "Marsupial mice—those little animals fertilize their little females with rivers of sperm, they literally flood them with semen. They sit on their hind legs and they flirtatiously display their testicles, testicles of an amazing size that attract the little females."

"Do you mind if I smoke?" As a precaution I showed him my cigar case with its three cigars.

"Are you smoking again? Go on, smoke as much as your eyes can stand," he said and drank another mouthful, this time without tasting. He shook his head thoughtfully. "The testicles are an amazing size, just imagine, they make up five percent of the total body weight of one of these marsupial mice. In our terms, that would mean your balls would weigh four kilos."

"Did you ever see this biologist naked?"

Kubin looked at me in surprise, his mouth took on a sardonic expression. "Good God," he said, "I hope you're not still hung up on that basic realism. Actually even marsupial mouse isn't quite right. Angela's botanist looks like one of those tailless water dingos." But by now Kubin had drunk so much, he couldn't tell me what a tailless water dingo was.

The Reichstag, wrapped

BELOW, THE TAXI WAS ALREADY WAITING OUT-side the house; on the balcony above stood Kubin, sou'wester on his head, yelling: "Mast and bulkheads broken!"

He was leaning far over the balcony railing, alarm-ingly far. "Be careful," I called up to him.

But he sang on into the stormy night: "Fourteen men on a dead man's chest, yo ho ho, and a bottle of rum."

The taxi driver asked: "Is he a skipper?"

"No. Management consultant. But his grandfather was a skipper. I've never seen him like this before. He used to sing Irish folk songs when he was drunk."

"Where to?"

"The Reichstag."

"Ah," said the driver, "the wrapping, don't get ex-cited, there's not much to see at night. Mind you, it's good for business. Hotels and boarding houses are full, yes, and taxis have been doing good business in the last two days."

"Is it all that bad otherwise?"

He nodded his bald head and looked in the mirror, but I couldn't see his eyes. Though it was night he was wearing sunglasses, pilot model, thirties style, the frame anodized in gold.

"Since Reunification we've been stuck in traffic jams. Building sites, redirected traffic, one-way streets all over the place, where there was nothing the day before. Now there's even a lake on Potsdamer Platz. A huge excavation with dredges, barges, and two tugs." The taxi clattered. We were driving over a temporary bridge.

"If there's mutiny on board a barge, maritime law applies. The traffic aggression that's built up here since Reunification, it's unbelievable. I came to Berlin twenty years ago, didn't want to go into the army. Berlin then was the place for dropouts and outsiders. A microcosm, walled in, well guarded. Now it's the boys wanting to make a quick killing that are coming here. I'm thinking of leaving."

"Where would you go?"

"Cologne or Hamburg."

Gusts of wind shook the car. A few drops of rain on the windshield. He turned on the windshield wipers.

"What do you do when you're not driving a taxi, I mean as a profession?"

"A lot of people ask that. They think I'm one of those taxi drivers with a Ph.D. I've a driving license, a taxi license, and two years of Romance languages and literature, and that's it. When I'm not driving a taxi I don't do much of anything, except read, go to movies, listen to music. And travel, Africa, the Sahara. I once wrote a little guidebook on the Sahara before it became so fashionable, but it's been out of print a long time. We're already at the barrier," he said, "from here you'll have to walk. I can drive round it, it won't make much difference though, except for the higher fare."

For a moment I wondered whether I shouldn't just ask him to take me to my hotel. But I was curious to see how much of the Reichstag had been wrapped. So I paid and got out.

The wind was cold and a fine rain was falling. I'd believed the weather report on the previous evening and for convenience left my raincoat at home. I now froze pitifully in the thin silk jacket I'd bought in Munich during the heat wave.

The Brandenburg Gate stood there as though lit from within. A few pedestrians were making their way wrapped in raincoats or capes. A car came, drove to the barrier and stopped. A car with an Italian license plate, a Lancia. My damp silk jacket was giving out a peculiar smell, strange, not like wool that smells so soothingly of wet sheep or the straw smell that comes from wet cotton. But the smell exuding from my jacket reminded me of slime, of a glandular secretion, it smelled almost gelatinous. I crossed the Straße des 17 Juni, named after the 1953 East Berlin uprising. The Lancia turned at the barrier railing and came towards me with headlights on, braked, the driver shouted something out to me. I went to the car and immediately said into the lowered window: "I'm not from here. Sono straniero."

"Ahh, Lei parla italiano."

"Solamente un poco."

He let fly in Italian. I only understood something about a fair and a night journey. And as he saw that I wasn't really understanding him he switched to German and spoke it well, if with a heavy accent, explaining that he was coming from a trade fair. "Here in Berlin. Leather goods. Didn't you read about it?"

"No," I said, "I just arrived today."

He told me he had some leftover stock. Two leather jackets. Display models. He had to get to Milan, tonight. Why take the jackets back with him? He opened the door, beckoned me to get in. For a moment I hesitated because I thought of all the stories I'd heard from travelers to Berlin in recent months: strangled hotel managers, ring fingers cut off, mugged tourists, assault, and murder. But the driver gestured at me to get in, and then there was that cheerful Italian laugh: "Prego, si accomodi," and so I got in the passenger seat. I'd hardly slammed the door shut before he drove off. The car moved a short distance into the dark area between two street lamps. I was alarmed and thought, this is a mugging after all. I quickly turned around, but there was nobody hiding on the back seat, there was only a black bag, though in the shape of a body. The Italian turned off the engine.

"Is cold?" He pointed to my jacket.

"Yes," I said. The smell exuding from my wet silk jacket was now really oppressive and I suddenly realized what this silk jacket smelled like—semen. I thought of the marsupial mice and decided that as soon as I got home I'd look in an encyclopedia to see from what orifice silkworms spun their thread.

"Actually it's forbidden," said the Italian, "unclean competition."

"Unfair competition," I said, and was immediately annoyed at my schoolmasterly correction. "I'm sorry."

"Why," he said, "it's important. Otherwise you keep making the same stupid mistake."

"Well," I said, "it's that friendly patience of the Italians, that's why they don't correct you when you try to speak Italian."

"When you speak, no. But they do when you sing."

"How's that?"

"You know the story about the American singer? The guy was singing for the first time at the opera, in Naples? He sings the first aria. The audience roars da capo. The American sings the aria again. The audience yells, roars da capo, the singer sings it again and again and again. The other singers are getting impatient, they want to sing their arias too. But the audience shouts: da capo. Finally the exhausted American singer asks: How many times am I supposed to sing this aria? Someone in the audience calls out: Until you get it right." He looked me over: "What size are you? Forty-two?"

"It depends, in Italian sizes more likely forty-four."

"Then these jackets will fit you perfectly. Good design, best quality leather, first-class workmanship." He reached back, pulled one jacket and then another from the black bag, showed me the label: Giorgione, and below it the size, forty-four, in fact. "I really wanted three - fifty for each jacket, you can have both for four-fifty. The actual price is twelve hundred, each, that is. I couldn't stay any longer at my hotel. You understand," he looked at me, smiled. I nodded and wondered why the more he spoke the less accent his German had. He must have lived in Germany for quite a while.

"I wanted to sell the jackets tomorrow in a boutique" he said, "but no hotel vacant, everything booked, the whole city. They're wrapping the Reichstag. People are going crazy. With us, they come to see weeping madonnas. With you, the Reichstag. This Christo," he laughed: "Dio mio, a magician. But I'm a good Catholic. I'm leaving tonight. So, both jackets for four-fifty."

"No," I said, "I don't need two jackets, it's June, these are fall jackets. Though it's raining. But what should I do with two leather jackets?"

"Sell them. You can easily ask two hundred more."

I shook my head.

"Good, then one. I want to sell both jackets today, this evening. Everyone knows there was a trade fair. I'll be driving all night, straight to Milan."

"The whole stretch," I asked.

"Yes," he said, "there's no one on the highway at night. I can, how do you say, rave up."

"No," I said and had to laugh, "it's rev up."

"Good," he said, "the one jacket for two-eighty. You're not wearing a coat. With this weather, the jacket. Rain." He pointed outside. The drizzle had in fact turned into rain, the wind flung it against the windshield.

"Well, leather isn't exactly suitable for rain either," I tried to show I knew about this. "And anyway, I don't have that much money on me."

"A credit card? We could drive to an ATM."

"I don't have any credit cards with me." Which was a lie. But if I was going to buy I wanted to bargain a little. I'm not completely clueless, I know Italy and the Italians, and I told him this, said, "Italy's the country I like traveling to the most and I really like Italians, their language, their fashions, their food. Tutto!"

This clearly pleased him, this tutto; he put his hand on my shoulder, said: "You speak very good Italian. OK then, two hundred and twenty marks for the jacket. See here, silk lining. Red, lined, elegant."

I felt the leather, soft, really soft to the touch. The

brand name Giorgione reminded me of Giorgione's painting: "The Storm." That's a painting I can keep coming back to, and each time I discover new details. For example the white bird on the roof of the house, really tiny, a stork, I think, sitting there while lightning flashes through the black thunderclouds. The jacket lining was really red, a dark red. I tried to examine the quality of the seams in the dim light, felt them. I said I'd once been a furrier. I had to explain to him what that was. Somebody who deals in fur and leather.

"Oh," he said, "an expert," pulled the jacket away from me and held it up: "You see, styled after il famoso barone rosse. Richthofen. Elegant cut. Old aviator design. Double-decker. Protects from wind and rain."

It looked good, especially as there was a triple-decker in the inner lining. At home my father had had a photo of Richthofen, whom he revered, up on the wall, and in this photo Richthofen was wearing a leather jacket that, I was certain, resembled this one.

"How much money have you got?"

I searched through my pockets. And thought, what luck, with this rain, this cold, getting a genuine soft leather jacket this cheap. I showed him my money: one hundred and seventy marks and a few pennies. Of course I didn't tell him that I had another hundred marks in my passport for an emergency. "One hundred and seventy marks, that's all. And then I can't even take a taxi back."

"Have you got a bus ticket?"

"No."

He gave me back four marks. "A good buy," he said. "Now I'm going on the autostrada and rave up."

"Rev up," I said.

He laughed: "German is very complicated: rev up! Yes, rave up! Lots of luck! Arrividerci!"

The Italians, I thought, are wonderful. They do their little deals, their little swindles, but always in such a way that you can still enjoy being cheated, and that's where I pulled a nice fast one on him. I said to myself and waved. That tutto, that softened him. He waved again, shouted addio and thank you, and drove off with tires screeching.

I put on the leather jacket, beautifully warm at last in all this wind and rain, at last. A really good buy, only one hundred sixty-six marks instead of twelve hundred. Almost a lucky number. Almost like that buy at the flea market on Lake Kleinhesseloh a year ago, where lost clothes were being sold and I bought myself a raincoat for a hundred and eighty, a Burberry as good as new, hardly worn, in the lining a label worked in gold from golden Basel: Conrad. High class for men. The previous owner must have had extremely short Swiss arms, because I had to have the sleeves of the coat, which otherwise was just right, let out a good four centimeters. While this jacket was a perfect fit, and it was warm, wonderfully warm.

The Reichstag: massive, heavy, rustling darkly. As in a dream, the hanging strips of cloth billowed in the gusting wind, dark and strange. The middle section was already wrapped, the four corner towers were still uncovered.

I walked along the yellow wire fence intended to keep the curious away from the work of art in progress.

Men in yellow rain capes guarded the fence. A few inquisitive people were walking, mute and muffled, by the fence; a woman struggled with her reversed umbrella, a man pulled a morose, wet, shaggy dog behind him on a lead, a little man in an old motorcyclist's jacket studied a billboard by a pile driver. Construction work I read on the sign.

I went further along the wire fence. My leather jacket was getting heavier in the rain, so heavy that, for the first time in years, I thought of the lead vest I once used during training, sprinting up the path to Richmond Castle, five, six times. The jacket had been light as a feather when I put it on, a typical Italian product. The leather had clearly only been tanned for sunny climes. Meanwhile my solid American leather shoes were also soaked. My feet were cold and wet. The storm rustled in the strips of grey synthetic material. In this lighting the color reminded me of the hideous bomber jackets of the People's Army. A man in a blue mining outift stood behind the fence, a yellow helmet on his head, around his hips a wide belt with thick snap links. I'd seen the men in the news yesterday, unrolling the massive strips of material like sailors on the yards of sailing boats.

I suddenly understood Kubin's cry: "Mast and bulkheads broken." He'll also have seen these pictures. I asked the man if he'd worked too on wrapping the Reichstag.

"Veiling," he instantly corrected me. "What gets veiled, at some point gets unveiled, at any rate that's what Christo says." He looked up anxiously at the billowing strips of cloth. "We had to stop work at noon. Regular gale-force winds. We were rocking up there like monkeys on bush ropes."

"Are you from Berlin?"

"No, I come from Rostock."

"Could you climb in the GDR?"

"No, only a little in the mountains along the Elbe. And of course factory chimneys."

"Factory chimneys?"

"Yes, under socialism we trained on chimneys. There was so little scaffolding. A deficient economy also has its advantages. So we worked with ropes from the top. That was powerful training. I once did repair work on a two-hundred-and-sixty-meter-high chimney. Now I'm independent. I specialize in chimneys, repair work: joining, replacing rungs. The money's good. I used to be a Hero of Labor, good for nothing except sticking in my cap. So," he said, "time to hit the sack. Have to get up early, at five."

I went on walking and suddenly I felt my joints ache with fatigue. I'd gotten up at five o'clock in the morning, raced through the book I was reading, *The Potato and Its Wild Relatives*, then gone to the State Library to look at the statistics for potato and sugar beet cultivation in the 19th century, flown in the afternoon from a warm summery Munich to a stormy cold Berlin, had plenty to eat and drink with Kubin, now I was running around at night in this leaden jacket and I said to myself, enough. I went down Unter den Linden heading for the Friedrichstraße station, in order to go to Bahnhof Zoo with the four marks the Italian had left me. Meanwhile the jacket had soaked up so much water it hung from my shoulders as if the side pockets were crammed with boulders. I tried to cheer myself up with the thought that the leather could be impregnated with a spray. Then it would be good for the cold but dry October days in Munich. Anyway, it still kept me warm. And I no longer smelled like the gelatinous excretion of silkworms, now I smelled of—what, actually? The smell reminded me of the secondhand dealer on the Eppendorferweg to whom I used to bring paper and cardboard when I was a child, and depending on the weight, get a few pennies for it. It was at the beginning of the fifties, at the time of the Korean War, scrap metal prices had risen sharply, when my father had called me. He was standing in the cellar, his feet wet, his trouser legs wet. He beckoned me to come closer and gave me a couple of slaps around the ear. Why did my father have to go and wash his hands at this basin in the cellar of all places, a washbasin that was normally never used? I'd removed the drain which was lead. Lead fetched the highest price, so I suppose you could say that the slaps were worth it. Exactly! It was this smell of paper from the secondhand dealer's cellar that I was carrying around now.

I was just turning into the Friedrichstraße when three men came towards me, all three in shiny bomber jackets, their heads not exactly shaved, but close-cropped. A practical haircut, I thought, while my hair hung in strands in my face. Why hadn't I let my wife cut it before I left?

"What you starin' at, you there," said one of them and came towards me. "You old bum." And the other said: "Dirty aldi." Then the first one gave me a feeble punch in the stomach. Water squirted out from my jacket as from a sponge. I winced and let out a faint cry although it had been more like a push and hadn't hurt. But the jacket had still torn. The three stared for a moment dazed, then horrified at the hole from which red was oozing. I pressed my hands to the mushy mess. I was stiff with surprise but felt no pain. The three ran, raced away. I slowly recovered from my shock, looked at my hands. They weren't red. The wet red inner lining was hanging out. I pushed it back into the jacket, a piece came off. Perhaps the man who slammed me had had a knife hidden in his hand, or a metal comb, or a key ring which, I'd heard, left terrible face wounds if you struck with it. So perhaps the bloated jacket had saved me from injury. But the rip in the jacket was big. A mended jacket, I tried consoling myself, would show that it was well worn. It would certainly take a lot of mending to patch this hole.

At the train station, finally dried out, I saw myself in the filthy pane of the swinging door that had probably not been cleaned since the Eighth Party Congress.

My dingy reflection also explained the words dirty aldi. The word was albi, and it meant the illegal Albanians sleeping out on the streets. The jacket wasn't just torn in two places, there was also something wrong with the collar. What a mess. My hair hung in strands in my face. I thought, lucky I'm not as dark as my reflection. I looked down at my jacket, it was literally frayed. No, it was in shreds. It was coming apart. I fingered it, pulled something away, a slimy mass like blotting paper. In school we tore blotting paper into pieces, chewed it into lumps and then spat it at the blackboard where it stuck like grey-white cookie mixture. The clump in my hand was black. I could pull off the inner lining in little red lumps. At least, I thought, looking at my fingers, the color doesn't come off, so it hasn't bled into the silk jacket. A young man walked by, gave me a friendly nod, and pressed a cigarette pack into my hand, blue, Gauloises, on it Mercury's helmet. This Italian was an ingenious fellow, I said to myself. I didn't even need to travel without a ticket. And the one hundred and sixty-six marks, they, my mother would have said, are an offering to the gods. Fear their envy. And lately things have gone well for me, even very well. No, I wasn't furious, wasn't bitter. And there were still three cigarettes in the pack. I pressed the pack into the hand of one of the homeless people, took off the disintegrating, dripping jacket, shoved it where it belonged—in a trash can—and ran up the steps to the platform.

The man next to Lysenko

THE NEXT MORNING I PHONED ROSENOW FROM my hotel. I gave him Kubin's regards and told him I wanted to write an article on the cultural history of the potato, could he give me Dr. Rogler's address.

"Rogler," said the voice and, after a moment's hesitation, "no, Rogler died."

"Oh dear! Kubin didn't mention that."

"He doesn't know. Rogler died five months ago."

"I'm sorry," I said. "I'd hoped to get some advice from Rogler."

"He'd certainly have been pleased to give it. But there's still Rogler's private potato archive."

"Can I get to it," I asked rather bluntly.

"It's in my old apartment. You're welcome to use it."

"That would be very helpful. I'm only in Berlin for a few days. Could it be soon?"

"Yes. We can meet today, around noon, if that suits you."

"Yes, that's fine. What do you suggest, where?"

"In the Paris Bar."

At one o'clock I waited at the Paris Bar and thought of what Kubin had said to me about the East Germans the previous evening, his speech already slurred: "The Ossies have a tremendous need to catch up, they always barge in where they think there's high society. And then they say the GDR wasn't too bad, strictly speaking, if only, yes, if only one could've been able to travel."

I'd imagined Rosenow, former member of the German Democratic Republic's Academy of Science, as a pale, bespectacled man with a receding hairline, in an old-fashioned suit with trousers of the type last worn by Khrushchev. But the man who now joined me at the table was wearing an elegant dark blue double-breasted jacket of the very best quality, with it a carefully-chosen tie that might have been designed by Matisse. Rosenow carefully placed a small cellular phone on the table and pulled out the aerial. To avoid any possible misunderstanding, I asked him if he was the potato expert's friend.

"Yes," he said, "I was. I was."

Rosenow—I'd say in his fifties—was suntanned, his hair streaked with grey, thick, even unruly, but strikingly well cut. I saw a faint, light strip at the nape of his neck. He must have had his hair cut just a day or two ago. The waiter greeted Rosenow as Doctor, rather than Herr Doctor, showing himself to be an authority on forms of address. Rosenow ordered grilled blutwurst, recommended it to me. Ordered himself a soda water.

"At least this," he said, "has stayed with me from the time of real socialism: no drinking when driving." To my question, what he was doing now, he replied, "Real estate at the moment." But freelance, he was working for a large company on commission. Without my asking he added: "Why not? It's typical in this society—everything's on the move and everyone's always worried about a crash—that's why they're after real estate. They all want property that will stay safe, but also plenty of moving around in all the other areas—travel, relationships, fashion. With us it used to be just the opposite— it was pointless to have real estate and so we had a static society with no moving around."

I was afraid I'd now have to listen to a long digression on the differences between a capitalist and a socialist society and so I quickly asked: "Do you know a variety of potato called Red Tree?"

"No," Rosenow laughed, "never heard of it. I was involved in cultural history, not the history of the potato. My area of research was city planning in Berlin and Brandenburg from the turn of the century to 1945. Really useful to me, as you can imagine, since the Wall came down." The waiter brought the water, set the glasses down, poured.

"And Rogler?"

"Rogler was an agronomist, then he specialized in the history of the potato. He spent years preparing an exhibition. He kept coming up with new ideas. Kept being turned down by the party bosses. That's how it was until the Reunification. He was the great authority in the field. Potatoes had grown close to his heart, if I can put it that way. Rosenow laughed, but it wasn't a derisive laugh. "Rogler's dream of a big exhibition was supposed to rehabilitate the potato, raise it to undreamed-of uses, especially here in the East where it's more widespread than anywhere else. Properly prepared, the potato was to be for the GDR what the noodle is to Italy. Comparable in quality, because our homegrown potatoes in the end had become watery, tasteless, in fact horrible."

Rosenow fished the two ice cubes out of his glass with a fork, pushed them onto the saucer, then took a sip of the soda water.

"A fanatic, Kubin said."

"Well, no, that's an exaggeration. I knew Rogler well. We were friends from way back. When I first met him he'd just been asked by the party to do this exhibition. That was after the Eighth Party Congress, with its push for liberalization. Rogler had taken this quite literally. He was convinced the GDR needed to be transformed by a cultural revolution. And that also meant getting away from sausage dishes, greasy cutlets, steamed potatoes. Our restaurant menus used to call them repletion side dishes. You have to let that word melt in your mouth: repletion side dishes." He drank some more water. I saw that it was still too cold for him, he held it a while in his mouth, then swallowed. He must have a delicate stomach, I thought, perhaps even gastritis.

"Yes," he said, "Rogler was convinced of it: above all, a change was needed not just in regard to property and possessions, but in awareness." Rosenow gave me a searching look.

"Gramsci," I said: "Only a change in habits, in feelings, in eroticism, in clothes and food will bring about a new society."

"Ahha," Rosenow laughed lightly, "I see there's also a curve to the left in your past. Yes, Rogler had read Gramsci, in fact learned Italian so he could since most of Gramsci's work hadn't been translated, at any rate not the criticism aimed at the cult of the proleteriat and that flat-footed Stalinist theory: Alone existence determines consciousness."

The waiter brought us the blutwurst and asked if we'd also like some French beans, lightly steamed, still crunchy. "Yes please, and you?" I nodded. "The GDR," Rosenow leaned back and said, "was wrecked by unfriendly waiters."

"What?"

"Yes," he said, "by the unfriendliness everywhere. If you've got a deficient economy, then you have to supply something else, more friendliness, more freedom, even for deviant sexual practices, and more leisure. But leisure with a good conscience. Under real socialism work stopped on Friday at noon. Even in factories. That's a fact. And as for the plan, the seven dwarfs saw to that. A dream. We're the laziest state in the world. Now that would've been propaganda. Instead, it was always ever onward. Until we ran out of steam. Well, I coped with the system, apart from some friction, but I was never in a situation where I had to prepare an exhibition like my friend Rogler."

The cellular phone beeped. He pressed the button, talked about a five-room apartment in an old building, also available for commercial purposes. Words like parquet, oak, tiled stove, stucco molding, laughing cupids at the corners of the ceiling, an inner courtyard. While he was talking I wondered what would be the quickest way to get him off his torrent of self-justification back to Rogler's potato archive.

"Yes," he said, "that's fine, I'll drop by in an hour." He put the cellular phone back on the table.

"What's the political angle on potatoes," I quickly asked him.

"Yes—what." He looked at me, slowly took a few sips of the soda. "Rogler could get really angry because in the GDR state intervention had greatly reduced the number of potato varieties. Rationalization through standardization is an economic boon, but aesthetically always an impoverishment, taste isn't taken into consideration. Those are Rogler's words, not mine. And then the socialist varieties of potato kept getting worse, no new varieties, in fact they were more and more tasteless. Substandard storage contributed to this, and long transportation on the decrepit rail system didn't improve them either. Rogler pleaded for a rigorous privatization of taste, as it were. Of course Rogler soon reached the limit of what the party leadership considered permissible. His exhibition wasn't forbidden, it was just not permitted. I also knew Rogler's predecessor, a follower of Lysenko. He was one of those who wanted to prove that Stalin had given the decisive tip on the frost-resistant potato."

I laughed.

"No, seriously, it was a matter of demonstrating that socialist potato cultivators, because they lived in a superior society, could also cultivate superior varieties of potato."

"Lysenko was really more of a comical figure."

Rosenow quietly put a piece of blutwurst in his mouth, chewed, swallowed: "I agree. But if you put a man with a gun next to Lysenko, then he suddenly becomes a scientist you take very seriously. Rogler came after the Lysenko disciple, who'd retired. It was, as is said, the time of the Thaw. Stalin lay in his Snow White's coffin, and his beard grew. And my friend Rogler wanted potatoes to illustrate socialism with a human face." Rosenow laughed a strange mirthless laugh and wiped the tears from the corners of his eyes. "Three times three years work," he said and took a breath,

"Rogler incorporated the party's new appraisal at the time, which changed again after three years. Three rejections. After that he refused to change his ideas. He just quietly worked on year in year out, and he was left in peace. Then the Wall fell."

"Why didn't Rogler try to put on the exhibition in the West after the Reunification?"

"He did." Rosenow pushed his plate aside. "He even got together with an ethnologist, a woman, from West Berlin. They were both looking for someone to donate money, sponsors, in other words. A big company that produced instant noodles and mashed potatoes in vacuum-sealed packages showed interest. And what did my friend Rogler have to say about that: That's just institutional mush. We already had that in the GDR, if not so good. But what really matters is to be able to taste the individual variety, each individual potato. Rosenow laughed and shook his head. "That's what he said to the managers with their instant noodles and packaged potato powder. And the people had actually been very well disposed to his plan for an exhibition. A few billboards for advertising? No. Some reference at least to the company that had just been taken over by the Americans? No. In fact, Rogler had understood neither the one society nor the other."

After hesitating a moment I asked: "What did he die of?"

"Not what you're thinking, he didn't take an overdose of sleeping pills. No, I think he was at peace with himself. Though towards the end I didn't see that much of him. We simply drifted apart a little, without any quarreling or animosity. And then I moved to West Berlin. Yes," said Rosenow and then, staring blankly for a moment, "he was genetically handicapped. His father died of a heart attack at forty-seven, his brother even earlier, and then he did, at the age of fifty-two. Heart attack. I'd even spoken to him on the phone the day before. We hadn't seen each other for quite a while. We phoned each other now and then. In the old days we shared a lot of laughs. We'd swap stories about the Academy, later about our experiences with the market economy that was such a mystery to us." Rosenow laughed. "For example I'd tell him about the rat lying quietly and dreamily asleep in the toilet bowl when the prospective buyer, a well-heeled investor, lifted the toilet lid in the completely renovated apartment in the old building. And Rogler told me how the unemployment office had tried to find him work in public relations for McDonald's. French fries do have something to do with potatoes. Rogler, of all people. No. He was already over fifty, and he knew absolutely nothing about public relations. Rogler told how, when he came into the office, the head of personnel could hardly restrain himself from laughing. Rogler could tell a story like that with a lot of self-deprecating irony. We'd spoken on the phone the day before his death. He was unusually serious and he said something very peculiar: You just have to strike tents like the Bedouin in the desert. Then the horizon's clear again. Strange, isn't it? That he should have come up with that, of all things? His sister cleared out his room, even the paintings, Russian constructivists. What'll I do with his potato archive, she asked me. All right, I'll take it. It's his personal archive. The rest, what he compiled for the Academy, is scattered. Some of it stored. Some of it vanished when the Academy was dissolved." Rosenow drank more of the soda water, repressed a belch. "Rogler was working on a completely crazy project. He wanted to set up a potato–taste catalogue."

"A taste catalogue?"

"Yes, the way there are taste catalogues for wine or tea. We were still living together back then. Rogler would be sitting there, tasting, pondering, searching for a word or a combination of words to describe what he was tasting. Just try describing the taste of potatoes. He wanted to differentiate exactly. Sometimes I'd run into him at night. I have to get up at least once because of my weak bladder. Rogler would be wandering up and down in the corridor and mumbling to himself. Puppish, no, young pup, youngster. Some new adjective for a variety of potato. He'd see me, back he'd go to his card index like someone walking in his sleep. A new world of taste was blossoming there." Rosenow drank the rest of the water and shook his head pensively. "Rogler was crazy in a wonderful way."

"And where is this private archive now?"

"It's still in the apartment where we lived together. You're welcome to the notes if you want. Frankly, there's not much I can do with them. Letting them gather dust in the attic out of piety surely can't be in Rogler's interest."

Rosenow insisted on paying, gave a good tip, and asked the waiter about his vacation plans while I was already waiting at the exit. He seemed relaxed, even serene. I thought perhaps he was glad to have found someone for this abandoned archive.

His cellular phone bleeped. "Yes," he said, "I'm coming. Later, maybe. Yes, all right, see you then."

We walked down the Kantstraße. He'd parked his BMW half on the sidewalk. "I'll give you my card." He wrote something on his card. "You'd really be doing me a favor if you collected the archive chest yourself. If I go, over there, I'm sure you understand, they're easily envious. A former colleague now lives in the apartment, Klaus Spranger, also pushed out of his job, he can give you the chest."

The fade cut

I DROVE TO THE ALEXANDERPLATZ AND FROM there took the U5 going to Hönow, to the East. A strikingly large number of colored bicycles were being taken onto the train, while in Munich at that time you saw mostly black bikes. Black was the fashion there for cyclists. The little girls wore earrings, the woman carried full shopping bags. A bag made of some synthetic material fell over, and four, five tins of margerine immediately rolled through the carriage. A boy crawled under the seats and picked them up. There was still the smell of that cleansing agent that I always associated with the GDR, that smell and, in winter, those constantly overheated rooms where people then always opened windows. That was the system's entropy. Opposite me sat two young men wearing Lacoste shirts. The little crocodiles looked as if they'd been stuck on later, they also seemed unusually large, and one of them even raised its tail. Wasn't it a test of the quality of these shirts that one couldn't remove these crocodiles? But perhaps I had a distorted view after yesterday's cardboard jacket.

I got out at Magdalenenstraße, there where the Red Army, coming down from the Seelower Höhen, had cut its way in. Here SS, Hitler Youth, and the territorial army defended house by house; block after block of houses were demolished by shellfire from Stalin's big guns and other Russian artillery. The new buildings were piled high in slab layers, the side streets also full of concrete monstrosities, with pebbly grey-brown walls that nonetheless still looked better than the filthy, blackened, naked concrete buildings in the West of the city. In a side street between some new structures, a very grand old building that had miraculously survived the war. This was the house where Spranger lived. On one side the Art Nouveau plaster on the facade had broken away in layers; where it still held to the brick-work it was full of bullet holes. From the number and shape of the holes you could tell behind which windows the snipers, German or Russian, had hidden in April '45.

The marble steps at the entrance were cracked, wide pieces were missing. Both hall mirrors had been broken off except for small corner fragments; up on the ceiling reeds hung out of a plaster amphora. The synthetic carpeting on the stairs was worn through, the wood frayed, on the walls children's drawings, little stick men, cars, trains, technological fossils, still with clouds of steam, a friendly smiling lady sun.

On the first floor Spranger's name was under two

others on the door. I rang. Shuffling footsteps. Shuffling right up to the door. Silence. Inside someone was standing listening, and outside I was standing listening. I cleared my throat, coughed exaggeratedly loudly. Silence. I knocked again. I said in a hoarse voice: "Hello." At this, the shuffling moved away again. Perhaps whoever was listening behind the door had just come from the bathroom, perhaps he'd been woken up from an afternoon nap. I stood and waited, not knowing whether to go or to stay. Finally I went slowly down the stairs, along the side street to the main street. The sun was shining. It was quite a bit warmer than yesterday. The people around me on the street didn't seem to be in a hurry. Above some shops a TO was still legible, painted over, but the color of the dark letters shone through. I wondered what this TO meant. Trade Organisation? In front of a perfume chain store stood a pathetic tree decorated with tiny candles alight now, in broad daylight. Instead of having a fairy-tale effect, the tree looked plucked bare and pitiful. A Vietnamese woman with a key was winding up plush dogs that waddled mechanically across the sidewalk, then suddenly leaped up, turned a somersault, landed on all fours again and went on waddling to the next somersault. She smiled at me: "Ten marks, for the kiddies." It sounded like: "for the fiddies." A few young people were standing by her talking to each other, in Romanian I decided, loud, even violent, and gesticulating. They were wearing those horrible stone-washed jackets and jeans, limp and grossly outsized. An elderly man carrying used plastic bags was being dragged along the sidewalk by a white-and-brown-spotted mongrel. Kubin, who maintained that the surface differences between East and West had long since disappeared, can't ever have been here.

A camper, painted white, was standing on Frankfurter Allee, round as a giant ostrich egg, a trailer, probably of Bulgarian or Armenian make. It had been refitted as a food stand. I ordered a curried sausage, a genuine East German one, the ketchup well warmed up and with plenty of curry. Next to me a girl was eating french fries with mayonnaise, thick and yellowish, no doubt the same mayonnaise as at Bahnhof Zoo, but I couldn't help feeling here it was the fat extracted from overfed chickens. I felt a slight nausea, threw the cardboard plate into the trash basket, and ordered a coke. The girl said: "They run over my Bruno yesterday. Didn't kill him not straight off, it didn't. He was laying there whimpering, he even got himself up on his front legs, like this, and his back legs dragging." She started crying, but went on eating the fries, dipping them into that yellow muck. "Didn't know what to do. Not until the firemen came. They gave him an injection. My boyfriend bailed on me, went off with a woman from the Ruhr. And now Bruno's gone, just like that."

I held out a paper napkin to her, but she didn't dab

her eyes with it, just wiped her mouth. Then walked off without a word, no thank you, no goodbye.

The man at the food stand said: "She's in a fine mess. And she had an abortion a month ago, her boyfriend clears off, and now no work, that's no kind of a life."

I went down several side streets and then back again to Spranger's house, climbed the stairs to the first floor, rang. Again the shuffling right up to the door. Silence. I put my head against the door to hear what was going on inside; at that very moment it opened, I stumbled head-long into the apartment, barged into an old man, almost collided with him. The old man said very quietly: "What is this, the charge of the light brigade?"

The man was unshaven, his hair, reddish-grey and long, hung in his face, his eyes were inflamed. His threadbare blue-and-white-striped bathrobe was tied with a filthy yellow cord.

"Are you Mr. Spranger?"

"Nah. Name's Kramer. Come in!"

He led the way into the kitchen. "Dr. Spranger'll be here in a minute," he said. "Tayka seat," he pointed to a kitchen stool.

He went to the refrigerator, took out a bottle of soda water, drank from it. His teeth were nicotine brown, lifeless stumps, probably false. The bridge of his nose was covered with a fine reddish-blue web of veins. "Doctor," he said and belched, "oops, Doctor Spranger's busy."

"What does he do?"

"Nada. Odd jobs, ever since you gave him the heave-ho." He sat down opposite me at the kitchen table.

"Well, I didn't give him the heave-ho, that's not my job."

"It was them professors, they kicked him out."

"I'm not a professor, I'm not an academic."

"So—well, Dr. Spranger was working on gypsy languages. Now they're all flat on their faces, those doctors. Can't do no harm, does it, if they get a taste of life. Would you like some water?" He held out the bottle. "You can have a glass, if you like."

"No thank you."

"Where are you from then over there?"

"Munich," I said, "but I don't think there is an over there anymore."

"That's what you think! Go to the john, you'll soon see there's still an over there over there. A genuine East German john. Lead pipes ripped off from Mr. Russia. Now the pipes are plastic. Just listen." In the distance I could hear gurgling. "That's the sausages tumbling through my room."

"Through your room?"

"Ten years ago in the winter the pipes bust, they put down pipes through my room. So I can hear just what the house shits out. Liquid or bone-hard. Whada you want with Dr. Spranger anyhow?"

I found myself remembering what Kubin, Hamburg citizen by conviction, had said: "Berlin is the sticks. You see it from the way people are driven by uninhibited curiosity, and then that need to talk. You know why? Because of the dialect, the unwieldy G gets filed down to the soft J, and the sharp, final capping S gets softened to something gentle. That's how you get this Berlin logorrhoea."

"So, whada you want?"

"I wanted to pick up Mr. Rogler's archive."

"Oh dear. Rogler's looking up at his potatoes from below now. You one of those potato researchers?"

"Not really. I want to write an article about potatoes for a magazine."

"So, from the pack of reporters," he said, "oh we like them; come on in, poke around like we're an outdoor zoo."

"No," I said, "I'm only interested in potatoes. Mr. Spranger apparently still has Rogler's archive."

"Archive, now that's rich, a cardboard box is more like it." He took another swig from the soda bottle. He held it out to me. "Sure you don't whan any?"

"What do you do, I mean as a profession?"

"Retirement. Barber. You want, I'll cut your hair. Ten marks. A third that is, at the most, of what you'd fork over somewhere else. Where do you get your cutting?"

"My wife does it."

"Figured as much when you came in." He got up, I could see his wrinkled penis under his bathrobe. He walked round me. "You can tell. Can do yah short back and sides. That always looks smart. Worked a lot with the People's Army, from majors upwards."

"No thank you."

"Once even cut Ulbricht's hair. Later you couldn't get anywhere near them. As long as they sent the General Secretary to the barber, that's when we still had socialism. That was when over there you all had your hair cut short as matchsticks. Korean scourge, right. I could cut that style too. Didn't want it here though—they wanted a part. A part does give the face some kinda direction, brings out the back of the head."

He walked round me, took a look. I could see he was dissatisfied with my haircut.

"Sure you don't want me to crop your hair, frayed as it looks. Hands off to those who don't know the job." He took some scissors from a kitchen cupboard and started snipping before my eyes, tiny little snips.

I thought of Rosenow and his hair, that good haircut.

"Did you cut Dr. Rosenow's hair?"

"Absolootly. Of course. Lived here for years. Now, should I?" He snipped in the air with the scissors.

"No, really not."

"Can do you a fade cut there at the back, there's a bald patch coming. A fade cut in the right place, your hair looks thicker right away. And ten marks, really that's nothing for you, but it's butter on my bread—my five hundred marks pension, that's really nothing."

For a moment I considered simply giving him the ten marks, but that would have been sure to insult him since he'd even cut the hair of Politburo members. He just had to be good. "I had a dentist," I said, "in Munich, a very good one who used to take care of the Politburo's teeth—bridges, fillings, and false teeth until he fled Berlin. The more some minor officials gave him a hard time, the more his daughter was bullied at school because of her bourgeois origins, the deeper he drilled into the healthy teeth of members of the central committee, laying bare all the nerves, until suddenly there was a second dentist there to watch him at work. On that very same evening he packed a suitcase and—the Wall hadn't yet been built—left for Munich. But by then he'd already worn down Ulbrich's molars to such an extent, they had to be taken out."

"Routine sabotage. That's right," said Kramer, "we had that. Always letting them have it, them at the top. That's how it'll always be. Thank God."

And again he snipped with the scissors at professional speed before my eyes: "And now what?"

"Well, all right then," I said, and would have liked to get up and run out. On the other hand, I'd save myself a lot of work if I could use Rogler's archive, not have the awkward business of ordering it from a library, and then very likely having to wait weeks because of the interlibrary loan.

He put a tea towel that smelled of dirty dishwater round my neck and began cutting, quickly, with a practiced hand, every now and then before my eyes cutting in the air with the scissors. When he leaned forward the bathrobe opened and I saw his penis, which looked pretty flabby.

"Give you a manicure next?"

"No thank you," I said, "really not."

"OK." He worked away at the back of my head, silent and concentrating, then he said: "Have you heard this one? An East German and a West German are sitting in a café reading a newspaper. A customer comes into the café. How do you know which is the West German?"

"I haven't a clue."

"The East German looks up from the paper, the West German doesn't."

"I don't get it," I said, "where's the joke?"

"That's just it," said Kramer, snipped and laughed, "the Wessies always ask, where's the joke. How do you get on with them in Munich?"

"Have you ever been to Munich?"

"No, in the past wasn't allowed, now I can't. What makes you go down there?"

"I just like it," I said defiantly, "just that—the mountains, the city, the lakes."

"So, and the people? They're a breed of their own, with those hats with their little shaving-brush tufts, if you're a barber they send up the adrenaline, and that *grüß Gott* of theirs, God greet you instead of hello, and that God be with you, *pfüat di* for goodbye."

"Well, you don't quite understand what they're say-ing at first." I fell silent, but then as he steadily snipped I remembered how, when I went to the barber's for the first time in Munich and was sitting there in front of the mirror, watching the barber cut my hair and trying to understand what he was telling me, I kept politely saying, ah yes, how interesting, exactly. Suddenly he pulled the towel away from my neck and said: Get out! He was throwing me out. The real problem then was to find a barber who'd finish cutting my hair. If you came to a barber with your hair half-cut like that he'd think you had lice, and that a colleague must have thrown you out because of it.

"They must be stark raving," he said, snipped in the air with the scissors, studied my haircut. "What you need is a part."

"What? Me? With that receding hairline?"

"Believe me. Take Axen for example. Studied him from close up. A Politburo member with an impossible haircut. They couldn't even show him abroad. So I gave him a part, then he looked presentable."

"No, look, please, definitely no part."

Someone was at the door, unlocking it. Footsteps in

the hall, a man came into the kitchen, mid-forties, reddish-blond hair, sparse in front and cut bristle length, long at the back and tied in a small ponytail. I thought, living under the same roof with this scissor-happy barber and wearing a ponytail, that shows character.

"This gentleman wants to see you," said Kramer, "I'm nearly finished. Just a moment," he pushed me back into the chair. Spranger watched as Kramer took a razor from a drawer in the kitchen cupboard, snapped it open, tested the sharpness of the blade on his thumb-nail, and then began shaving the nape of my neck. It made me feel sort of ill. Spranger was also watching intently, not saying a word. The blade glided gently, I could hardly feel it. "Finished," said Kramer, carefully took away the dishcloth, shook it out onto the kitchen floor. He took a hairbrush from the drawer, brushed away the little hairs from my shirt collar.

I gave him twenty marks. "Thanks."

"And a tip, sir, that's classy."

The out-of-tune grand piano

SPRANGER LED ME INTO A ROOM THE SIZE OF A small gym. In the middle of it a concert grand piano stood stacked with books, newspapers, magazines, and all kinds of clutter. Apart from this, the room was empty except for a stool, an armchair, and a high cupboard. It smelled of stale smoke, and then there was another smell, only faint and that I liked, but I didn't know what it was.

"Please take a seat," said Spranger and pointed to the chair, a Biedermeier chair, the backrest in the shape of a lyre.

Spranger pulled a silver-stemmed pipe from the side pocket of his stained blue jacket, which he must have already filled because he calmly lit it. I was immediately struck by Spranger's relaxed movements, his slow, reflective way of speaking. He sat on the arm of the leather chair and, pipe in mouth, read what Rosenow had written in tiny handwriting on the card: a question, how was he, and did Spranger still have bills to settle, and had a Mrs. Stewens shown up, then the request to hand over

Rogler's archive to me, also regards to Kramer. Spranger sat on the arm of the chair like Schiller on his donkey in Karlsbad. If I remember the drawing correctly, Schiller sits sideways, his legs dangling, on the donkey and pensively smokes a long-stemmed pipe.

Spranger took the pipe out of his mouth and said: "Good." And then there was a pause that got longer, so that I felt it was up to me to say something: "Do you play the piano," I asked, the word piano, in view of the massive instrument, unwittingly giving my question an ironic twist.

"No. I don't play. I took the piano over with the room from Rosenow."

"Did Rosenow play?"

"No, he didn't. The piano belonged to the apartment's previous owner, a businessman. The piano is an orphan. And he didn't play either. It stood here at the entrance in April '45. Presumably from an opera house or a large theatre in the East: Stettin, Tilsit, or Danzig. It had been taken by horse and cart on the flight from the Red Army, until it was left here, at the entrance, well packed and covered with a tarpaulin. A Russian colonel billeted in the house then had it brought up into the apartment. It must have been subjected to some incredible hammering. It's completely out-of-tune, painfully so. It already has a quality of its own that a composer could use. Would you like some coffee or tea?"

"I'd like some tea, please."

Spranger left the room, came back again, and pulled the sliding door to the adjoining room shut. "My bedroom," he said. I heard him cross the hall and talk to the barber in the kitchen. Perhaps, I thought, he'll be praising me now, someone who came from the West and was willing to let himself be given a smart haircut and in doing so increase a meager pension. But then I heard them both laughing and the suspicion dawned on me that they were in cahoots. They're laughing at the Wessie coming here and letting himself be shorn like a mooncalf. On the other hand, that didn't seem like Spranger. I went around the room looking for a mirror. The walls were bare except for an oil painting, a blue sphere penetrating a red field, above it two white stripes. I was about to look at it more closely when I distinctly smelled what I'd already noticed when I came in, it was the smell of turpentine. It smelled as if it had just been painted. The colors were subdued and yet, here was the secret, they were radiant. I listened. Voices from the kitchen could still be heard. I carefully lifted the painting from the hook. It was painted on wood. On the back there was a small stamp with Cyrillic script. A painting from the twenties? For years I'd been looking for a painting for the white wall in my study, and I'd always imagined it would have to be a painting by a Russian Constructivist. But every attempt to acquire one had failed because of the price. I carefully hung the pic-

ture back on the wall. Against the opposite wall stood a
narrow wooden cupboard that reached the ceiling. I
carefully pulled open a few drawers. Inside were cassettes. The drawers were labeled: Romany, fairy tales,
songs, instrumental, violin, zither. They were probably
recordings made for Spranger's research. There were
also cassettes on the piano with titles like: The Chicken,
The Goose, Bittern, Hunting, Washing and Song, The
Hedgehog, The Violin, The Rose. Next to The Rose
cassette I discovered a hole in the pitch-black lacquered
lid of the piano, a hole as if from a bullet, round, the
edges a little splintered. Leaning against one of the
pompous piano legs stood two paintings, collages, with
newspaper cuttings in Cyrillic script, wrapping paper,
jumping jacks in oil, also constructivist.

I heard footsteps in the corridor and went quickly
back to the painting on the wall.

Spranger came in with a tray, with his elbow pushed
aside a heap of books on the piano, and put the tray
down. He poured the tea. "Would you like sugar or
milk?"

"Yes, milk, please. Do you collect Russian constructivists?"

"No," he said, "Rogler collected them. Already before the collapse of the USSR. Then in 1990 many paintings came. Mostly from old communists who sold them
for dollars to survive. And then of course many paintings
from the storerooms of Russian provincial museums,

stolen as well as officially sold. Do you want to buy one?"

"If I could afford it, gladly." I pointed to the blue sphere. "This painting looks old, but smells as if it's just been painted. Has it been restored?"

"If you like, yes."

"Beautiful. A Lebedev?"

"Could be, it's not signed," said Spranger. "Do sit down," Spranger pointed to the old light brown chair from which the leather was peeling as if from sunburn. I sat at a slight list on the worn-out springs. "Do you mind if I smoke a cigar?"

"Not at all," he said and followed the all with a little smoke ring.

"Fantastic," I said. I also tried to blow a smoke ring and I succeeded, nicely round and firm, then another, but one which already came apart, stretched out and crooked, as I exhaled. "For at least two months now I've been smoking again," I said, "and now and then I practice blowing smoke rings. An uncle of mine could blow three rings that went through each other. A big one, then medium-size, then lastly a small one. The last two flew through the big one, their sequence reversed. The last became the first."

Spranger smiled. "You could perform in a circus."

"I don't know, it's more for domestic use." We sat there for a moment, he drew the smoke from his pipe, I from my cigar, and we blew smoke rings.

"Smoke rings belong to a time," said Spranger,

"when smoking was a calm activity, not today's hectic smoking. Just take a look at people who smoke cigarettes, just a quick smoke. The pipe or the cigar on the other hand, smoking them is an art and smoke rings are their visible product. From what I smell, you're smoking a good brand? Havana?"

"Yes. A Cohiba. Can I offer you one?" I held out the case.

He hesitated, I could see he wanted to politely refuse as there were only two cigars left, but he then did reach out, a little too quickly, a little too hastily, which he himself noticed because he braked the movement at the last moment, carefully took the cigar from the case, and said, as if to distract from his overeager gesture: "A nice case. Genuine tortoiseshell."

"Yes, but murdering tortoises is banned. It's from my grandfather."

He sniffed the cigar, lit it by turning it slowly in the match's flame, briefly drew on it, blew on the glow until it was even. A connoisseur.

"Are you writing a botanical or a socio-cultural work on the potato?"

"More social and cultural, but in fact I really also want to write about an uncle of mine who could taste the different potato varieties."

We sat there for a while silent and smoking, concentrating completely on the taste and as if bonded by the gentle clouds of fragrant smoke.

"Rosenow told me that Rogler had compiled an index on the tastes of different potato varieties."

"Yes, a strange undertaking. Rogler didn't want to describe taste by comparison, but, arising out of the nature of the thing, by a new nomenclature. Yet already from the beginning there was something wrong with the theory. I don't think you can invent a new taste any more than you can a new awareness. For that it takes a kind of libidinous chaos. You can't think up something like that at a desk. A word has to suddenly surface, like this," Spranger snapped his fingers, "then it's like a bridge, you cross it and you see something different or you taste something new."

"Interesting," I said, "Rosenow also said that, that what Rogler was planning was a GDR project."

"Rogler had something else in mind than I did!" Spranger said this with a sharp emphasis on the *something else*. "Rosenow's criticism isn't mine. He had secretly prepared himself for the Wall eventually falling, which no one reckoned would happen so soon. His entire career was based on an eventual reversal of property ownership. You could say that he raised land registration to the level of academic research, no one knows more about the subject, at any rate not in the area of interest to property speculators, which is South Berlin, there where the new airport's going to be. Schönefeld or Sperenberg. A battle of real estate dealers, depending on which site they placed their bets. Experts for and against. I suspect the airport will be in Sperenberg, in the wilderness. And do you know why? Because Rosenow has bought himself two hundred thousand square meters of forest and heath there. Not in one piece, but like on a chessboard. That way he covers a huge area. No matter where they go, if they build in Sperenberg, they'll hit Rosenow property. He suggested I buy a few thousand square meters with him. A surefire investment, he said. A square meter at one-fifty. Ten thousand square meters for a piddling fifteen thou. That's how he talks now. Take thirty thousand, he said. And where would I get that kind of money? All he did was laugh and say: Go to the bank. You have to change your ideas, he said. But that's just what I find difficult. Think about them, yes, but why immediately change?"

For a moment we smoked in silence. Somewhere in the house a radio was on. An announcer, incomprehensible, then music, something classical.

"Was Rogler married?"

"Yes, but divorced, long ago. I never met his wife. He had girlfriends. Finally there was a woman who came often. He wanted to set up an exhibition over there with her. Very much a woman from the West, West in the sense of how she dressed, the way she presented herself. Our Figaro, who has a sharp eye for people, said: Beautiful, rich, good head on her shoulders, got everything, gets everything, but she also wants everything, that's her one fault. Kramer thought they were having an affair. I don't think the relationship went beyond planning the exhibition. They were so different. They embodied the clichés of East and West. Rogler didn't care a bit about clothes, wore typical Vietnamese sandals, shiny trousers, old baggy pullover with deer on it knitted by a great-aunt. Whereas the woman—as I said, a strikingly beautiful woman—wore silk dresses and despite the protection of species, snakeskin shoes, though she claimed, when I asked her, that they were imitation leather. I know something about snakes, I learned it in Romania from the gypsies. And as for her hairstyle, even Kramer didn't dare offer her a new one." Spranger laughed for the first time since we'd been sitting here together.

"Did Rosenow live in this room?"

"Yes, until just two years ago. Then I moved in and that's how, as I said, I took over the piano."

I got up and went to the piano, ran my hand across the lacquer, in really good condition, and then as if I'd just discovered it between the papers and the books: "There's a hole here in the lid."

"Yes. Our Figaro should really tell you that story. Kramer, you see, has been living here since '46."

"Fine," I said, "but he's already cut my hair, and I definitely don't want a manicure."

"I quite understand. So, the businessman who

owned the house in '45 had the maid's room. A Russian colonel, his adjutant, and two guys were billeted in the other rooms. The colonel must have been an excellent marksman with the revolver, he was in the habit of shooting a champagne glass out of the businessman's hand. Sometimes the businessman even put the glass on his head. Not sadism. Well-oiled, they played Wilhelm Tell and son. But on one occaasion the colonel was so drunk he missed, he didn't hit the businessman but the open lid of the piano on which an NKVD officer was in the midst of playing a mazurka. After that the colonel was sent on disciplinary transfer to Murmansk. But apart from being hideously out-of-tune, the piano's intact. As you can see though, it's only used as a place to dump things. Sometimes when I'm wrapping bunches of tulips in cellophane at the wholesale florists, cutting the stems with the shears, I think, sell the piano. Once I was even about to, I had an offer. It was to be picked up. But the night before I had a strange dream. As it was being carried down the piano plunged down the stairs. I was standing at the top and could see everything as if from a box at the theater. The piano had slipped from the grasp of the moving men, and the strap broke. The piano plummeted down the stairs. What came out of its splintering, ringing, wire-ripping, gigantic, toothy mouth was a shrill dissonant shriek— horrified and despairing. I was woken by my own cry.

That very night I decided to keep the piano. I said to myself, the piano belongs in this room, after a long wild journey it found its home, here."

He puffed on the cigar. "Damn it," he said, "talking about this piano now my cigar's gone out. If you don't mind, I'll finish it at my leisure later." He carefully brushed off the ash and put the cigar in the ashtray.

"Come! I'll show you Rogler's room." We went down a long dark corridor, there were shelves on the walls covered with strips of cloth. There was a smell of old clothes, shoes, and damp paper. It reminded me of my Italian cardboard jacket. At least I had the satisfaction of having knocked the smooth Italian swindler's price down so much that even for him it won't have been a very good deal.

"A heating technician moved into Rogler's room," said Spranger, "he's only here now and then. He's away on a job in Brandenburg. Otherwise not much has changed. You can take the box with you right now."

The room had a high and wide window, but it was still dark because of the wall of the house opposite, which was close. Here there was also a smell of turpentine. There was a cupboard, a bed, a wooden plank on two trestles serving as a desk, and an easel on which there was a half-finished painting, simple colored geometric figures, between them a collage of newspaper cuttings, all yellowed and in Cyrillic script.

"Are the newspapers old," I asked.

"No," said Spranger, "that's tea, ironed in."

"But the text?"

"Also not. 1988. There are hardly any differences. Descriptions of how the West is rotting, of constant progress in the socialist society of the USSR, ever onward, onward to the point of exhaustion, in 1928 as in 1988. I cut the collage in such a way that no name appears, in other words no Shevardnadze, Bush, or Baker. This is Constructivism's late revenge on Stalin's functionaries who opposed it."

"Do you sell the paintings, how can I put it . . . ?"

"As genuine? No. I sell them to people like yourself, I don't care then what they do with them. Well, that's not strictly true. It's fun. It's my answer to the Reunification."

"I don't get it."

"Forgery's the game. The result, replication. Vietnamese sell you Armani suits or Swiss watches from Leningrad. Painting calms my nerves." He looked at me, "Please don't think that I'm one of those who are nostalgic for the old system. I literally sighed with relief when our senile old men's regime was demonstrated out of existence, but I don't belong to those jubilant at being one nation. Here, by the way, I completely agree with Rogler. We wanted something other than the Treuhand privatizations. The conditions for that weren't bad. You Westerners are the formalists, we were the informal ones, we were the pathfinders in this ideologically fossilized system, excellent handymen, improvisers. Fighters in a small way against prescription and spoon-feeding, subversive resisters."

This was now the second political science lecture I'd been given today and I tried to divert Spranger from further excursions and bring him back to Rogler and potatoes: "Where did Rogler eat and work?"

"Here, at this desk, when he wasn't in his room at the Academy. But it wasn't all so dismal then, don't think that. As I said, the Constructivist paintings hung here, not the very best, but nevertheless. Rogler's sister had inherited them and immediately sold them to a Munich gallery for a ridiculous sum."

"If you don't mind my asking: Why are you specifically copying the Constructivists?"

"For a very simple reason: I can't paint." And when I laughed, he said: "No, I really can't. Unless you're color-blind, Constructivists are easy to copy, you can even paint completely new pictures, your own, without an original, it's folk art in the good sense of the word. And I earn a little by it."

"And your academic work?"

"I was dumped, or put more delicately, down-sized. I'm fifty-three. I now cut fresh flowers—roses, carnations, tulips—and wrap them in cellophane. I'm quite satisfied. I've plenty of time to think at work, and I work a lot in the open air. If in the evening you see a Tamil selling roses in restaurants and bars, it's quite likely that I bathed them in a preservative that morning. They may well then hang their heads, but they don't lose their petals. They're, as it were, glued on from the inside. Simply amazing, the things that have been invented in the West. That by the way is the box there. Used for moving." Spranger pulled up the lid. Pulled out a few books, some boxes of index cards, then a small beautiful old cherrywood box, tongue-and-grooved, with an ebony inlay in the shape of an amphora for the keyhole. "Here's the taste catalogue," he said. He opened the little box which wasn't locked. Inside were small pale blue index cards, neatly written on and in alphabetical order. I leafed through a few cards and read names such as: Bettina, Clara, Spunta, Bellaria, Veronika, Imperial Chancellor, Rat, Monalisa, Sissy, Binje.

"This, I think you can say without exaggeration, is Rogler's life's work, aside from all the other data and files, pictures, and photos that he collected. I always thought the snakeskin shoe woman would come and collect the archive. But she never showed up again. What's more, she wasn't at Rogler's funeral. Instead there was a student. She cried as if they were burying her father."

"What student?"

"She was writing a study of the potato in German literature. It could be of interest to you. I must still have her phone number. The potato in Strittmatter and Arno

Schmidt. He lifted the moving carton and pressed it into my arms. I was surprised how heavy it was.

It took me almost an hour to get a taxi. First I waited outside the house, but as no taxis came through this side street I dragged the box to the main road. Strange—empty taxis simply drove past me. I waved. Finally a taxi stopped, a Mercedes. The driver got out, his stomach bursting out of GDR railway-blue trousers with sewn-in creases. He stood in front of the moving carton, said: "No way, I'm not a moving van."

"Couldn't we put the box in the trunk?"

"How—the lid isn't gonna shut. You gonna have to take a van."

I offered him ten marks extra if he'd take me with the box to Meinekestraße. Near Kudamm. He thought about it—"OK." As I was lifting the box he tore it from my hands: "Now hang on, it won't fit like that." He opened the box and began unpacking, throwing folders, slides, books, and bundles tied together into the trunk.

"What's this then," he asked and began rummaging through a bundle of papers, "secret material or what?" He held up a photocopy, "Ahha," he said, "these is blueprints."

"Blueprints of potato genes, I suspect—careful, this is important material."

"Ahha." Now he was thoroughly suspicious. "Deep-sixing that too. Is it a going-out-of-business sale, or what?" He brutally squashed the cardboard box, slammed the trunk lid shut. Went around to the front of the car cursing, sat at the wheel, kept staring into the rearview mirror. "Where to?"

"Meinekestraße."

"Matter of fact, I'm sposed to be off already," he said.

"But you did stop." I tried to smile into the rearview mirror.

"How's I sposed to know you had all this junk, and then top it all off with a long ride?"

"Other taxi drivers are pleased when they get a long ride."

"Not when they's sposed to be off."

"Is it your cab?" I asked in order to distract him.

"Yah've got to be kidding. Where the hell am I sposed to come up with sixty thou? Why dayah keep screwing with your collar like that, you got lice?"

"No. I had my hair cut."

Without asking he lit a cigarette, a horribly stinking one. Caro, Stalin's revenge, I thought.

"They're cleaning house here, bucking it all o'er there," he said. "You get it, everyone's coming here, cleaning us out."

"Uh-huh," I said.

"What do you mean, uh-huh?"

"Let me finish what I'm saying."

"Hold it," he said, "don't yah talk to me like that, or yah can get on outta here."

"Good. I want to get out."

He drove on. Clearly he hadn't counted on this. He peered in the rear mirror, and now and then he turned around, "I'm stopping when it suits me, and when the traffic lets me. Got it?" He turned red, no, violet. "Got it," he yelled.

"Stop! Stop right now!"

"Who do you think you are! You dummy back there, shut your trap!" Next to us was a Volkswagen, a family inside stared at us. My driver raised a fist.

The traffic lights turned red.

"Stop right now," I yelled. "You street fascist!"

"That does it," he yelled. He rammed the brakes so that I flew forward, pulled over to the right, and, astonishingly agile given his weight, jumped out of the car, tore the door open, and yelled: "Get outta here!" Behind us a hate-filled, demented honking began. I got out, wanted to take out the box. "Get your paws offa my trunk," Fatso cursed. He tore open the trunk, slammed the cardboard box down on the roadway, flung the photos, books, cassettes, slides he'd thrown into the trunk onto the asphalt.

"I'm going to file a complaint."

"You know whatya can do. Go fly a kite. Got it? And don't show up here again," and he flung himself into the driver's seat.

A car behind drove slowly towards me, nonstop honking; I felt the bumper against my calves. They've finished work, I said to myself, the workers want to go home, too bad, I crouched and swept everything together, crammed papers, books into the box. Behind me honking, people cursing at me from their cars. By the roadside a child was being punished with a slap, probably something to do with me, but don't ask me what.

The taxi drove off. Its number: B-St 345. I searched for my ballpoint, tried imprinting the number into my mind, dragged the cardboard box to the sidewalk while the approaching cars drove over index cards, books, pages, photos. When the light turned back to red I ran to the driver of a VW, asked him, would he be a witness.

"Nah, I don't want to get mixed up in anything." He quickly rolled up the window.

Every time the lights turned red, I gathered up pages, photos, books; when the lights turned green, jumped back onto the sidewalk. Behind me the screech of spinning tires.

An old man came and helped me gather up the pieces I'd thrown onto the sidewalk. A young woman brought me two pages that had blown across the street. "A bit dirty," she said, and wiped one side with a tissue.

"Thank you," I said, "thank you." I stood at the roadside next to the cardboard box, Schädel's *World Chronicle* in my hands. Bauhin's first description of the potato, Phytopinax, a rarity of the first order, 1596, the back of the book now broken. I leafed through it. Bauhin, I'd read just two days ago, was the first to assign the potato to the Solanaceae, the nightshade family. I put the book back in the box and thought of my desk, my quiet study in Munich, I cursed the moment when I'd agreed to write something about the potato and allowed myself to be taken away from my work. Instead of writing the beginning of my book, which I was sure I'd have found by now, here I was in East Berlin, involved in a totally crazy affair. In vain I tried to flag down a taxi. It was as if all taxi drivers had come to an agreement not to take me. When I waved they gave me a quick glance and drove on. Once a private car stopped, the man asked me, "How much a pack?"

"What pack?"

"What brands have you got?" He pointed to the cardboard box.

"That's not cigarettes. That's a potato archive."

The driver indignantly shook his head, tapped his forehead, and drove on. I stand a short distance away from the cardboard box, as if it doesn't belong to me. I wave to another taxi. And it actually does stop. The driver, a Portuguese, lifted the box into the trunk; on the way he cheers me up. "There are all kinds of people. Friendly and somber."

What a strange word from the mouth of a Portuguese, and so curiously pronounced, gentle and soft, it didn't sound somber.

"Do you know Pessoa," I asked him.

"Yes, of course, sir."

"Before I flew to Berlin I was reading the *Book of Unrest*. One sentence stayed with me: Suddenly, like a scream, a wonderful day shattered."

"I can't remember the sentence," said the taxi driver, "but I can tell you the sentence in Portuguese: E súbito, como um gritto, umformidável dia estilaçou-se."

That's how in that soft melodic intonation, just before bleak Alexanderplatz, a hibiscus blossomed.

Nightshade

WHEN I COME TO BERLIN I USUALLY STAY AT the Hotel Imperator, an apartment in an old building with creaking parquet floors and twelve rooms. In the rooms, in the corridor, in the breakfast room, in the reception hang pictures and graphics by contemporary artists, some are dedicated to the owner of the hotel, as also are sheets of music by Stockhausen and American jazz musicians. It was in such hotels, I like to imagine, that Isherwood, Auden, and Spender must have lived in the twenties. And I feel good here.

The hotel owner was sitting at her desk, her dog at her feet, snout on his front paws, suffering in his eyes.

"What's the matter with him?"

"A terrible night," she said, "yesterday he broke a tooth on a bone. I have to go to the vet later. He's getting a crown." She pointed to my cardboard box. "Have you been shopping at Aldi's?"

"No, this is a potato archive."

She's known me for years, knows my wonderful circle of acquaintances, knows about my remarkable research, she is the soul of discretion and on this occasion too she didn't ask further questions. But I'd no sooner turned my back to her when she cried out: "What have they done to you?"

"A cab driver threw me out of his taxi, he flung everything onto the street—books, notes, slides."

"No. I mean your hair."

"What?"

She laughed, "You look as if you'd fallen down the stairs."

"Yes. I was at the barber's."

"They've completely messed up your hair. Wait, I'll give you a hand mirror, you'll see for yourself."

In my room I put the cardboard box on the table and went to the mirror above the washbasin. In front my hair was well cut. Holding the hand mirror over the back of my head I saw three stripes slanting from bottom left to top right, not parallel, but cut so they spread slightly, in other words cut like rays. That pig had really messed up my hair. And collected twenty marks for doing it. Of course this was no accident. The words routine sabotage came back to mind. Perhaps it was my jacket, Kramer will have seen it was sinfully expensive precisely because it looked so plain. I stared at the back of my head in the mirror: I looked grotesque. And ridiculous. Even in the dim light here I could see my scalp. I tried combing the three stripes together. Impossible. My hair was too short. Spranger, whom I'd thought so pleasant, must have seen this, and what made me even more bitter was that he'd then taken a Havana. On the other hand, I told myself—anticipating my wife's attempts to calm me down—it could be that Spranger never really saw me from the back. I couldn't remember ever having turned my back to him. Even in the kitchen when he was waiting for me while Kramer was shaving my neck he was standing in front of me—if I remember correctly. I'd have to buy myself a cap. A knitted one would be best, one that I could pull down low over the back of my head. Yesterday with the wind and rain it would have been quite suitable, but in today's heat it would look as if I wanted to play the rapper from the ghetto.

I went into the hotel kitchen, got myself a beer from the refrigerator, ticked it off on the list provided. As I was on my way back across the hall, a young man came out of a room behind me: "Hello."

"Hello."

I walked ahead of him down the hall, my right hand over the back of my head as if I'd just banged it. In the room I started unpacking the cardboard box. I'd crammed everything into it, bent and crumpled, just as I'd grabbed it off the street. I searched, rummaged, my blood ran cold: the little cherrywood box with the taste catalogue was missing. All I found among the papers was one pale blue index card that must have fallen out.

The heading for the card from the taste catalogue was typed:

*BAMBERGEHÖRNDEL, also Bamerghörndl,
shape elongated, often crooked, numerous eyes, almost paired, tender skin, easily removed, like paper. Cooked, eaten like a vegetable, nutty taste,
bland, tender, not crumbly. Baked in olive oil:
criscrunch. In butter: crusround.* (The neolo-
gisms were underlined in red.) *Offshoots. Late.
(September). Rare. Cultivated in the Franken region. Intensive cultivation. Possibly a very early
hybrid from the time of the Nürnberg apothecary
gardens.*

I went to the breakfast room where the phone was
and called the taxi depot, gave the cab number, B-ST
345, and was shunted from one person to another. A
woman's voice said there was no record of such a taxi
number.

"Impossible," I said, "I remember the number. The
driver drove off with a box of academic file-cards."

"I'm sure the driver will report it or hand it in at the
Lost and Found."

"Who knows, the driver was a rather unpleasant
sort."

"I'm sorry, but we don't have a record of the number. You must have made a mistake," said the woman.

"No, the number's correct. I'm absolutely sure of
that. Three, four, five, that's not hard to remember."

"I'm really sorry. But perhaps it was a car that

didn't have a license. That's happened before. Unfortunately I can't help you here. Why don't you try the Lost and Found Office?"

"Are you from West Berlin?"

"No, a real East German sort, a one hundred percent Ossie. Why do you ask?"

"No particular reason, and thank you for your trouble." I hung up and went back to my room. What a shitty day. I couldn't see that repulsive creep ever taking the index cards to the Lost and Found place. He'd probably stop somewhere, dump the contents of the little box in a rubbish bin, and then give the cherrywood box to his wife for her sewing things or bills. Biedermeier. Or he'll sell it. The thought of Rogler, of all his laborious work that had taken years and was now in the hands of that scumbag tormented me although I only knew of Rogler from the stories I'd been told, I didn't even know what he looked like. I searched among the papers, the books in the cardboard box for more pale blue index cards with taste classifications that might have fallen out. Nothing. Only tattered photocopies and any number of white index cards thrown together, hand-colored charts of potato varieties. The potato in art: caricatures, reproductions of paintings in which potatoes were depicted, van Gogh, "The Potato Eaters," Max Liebermann. One picture showed Frederick the Great with peasants loyally handing him potatoes and another of him at table eating a dish of potatoes before astounded peasants. Among these illustrations was a large photo of a woman: a dark haired woman who seemed to be excitedly, even anxiously haranguing the photographer—regular features, dark eyes, mouth open, a reflection of light on the lower lip, the left, dark eyebrow lightly raised like a wing, in her left ear a little stone, a tailored jacket, black, with light pinstripes. A soft shadow in the middle indicated round high breasts, over them a pendant—a silver coin set in gold, on it, I was pretty sure, Athena with her helmet. There was something businesslike about the woman, and I thought this is how the woman whom Spranger had described as so typically from the West might have looked.

I collected the large white index cards from the box, they'd been flung in, bent, some marked with the pattern of the tires, index cards with notes, sketches, quotations, neatly inscribed, typed or by hand, a small black handwriting that reminded me of delicate bird footprints, the notes easily legible:

> *They belong together, tomato, tobacco, potato, all nightshade family, as also belladonna, in antiquity gave its name to one of the Fates, Atropa, the Mandragora or Mandrake root, caused madness and visions, belladonna gave the pupils of beauties wicked and blackest hellish depths, henbane. Nightshade, nightmares, aphrodisiac, dreamtime.*

Tobacco: *Neurotoxin (nicotine) for industrious citizens (Calvinists). Tobacco came via Holland and England. A neurotoxin that stimulates the mind and at the same time calms the body. So you can sit stimulated but calm at your desk: businessmen, academics, writers. Ex fumo dare lucem. Smoking lets you forget hunger and keeps you awake. The deeper reason why smoking increases during wars, since the Thirty Year War.*

The tomato: *Also paradise egg, love apple, etc., comes from the Andes via Mexico to Italy. Here they meet as if they had long awaited each other: olive oil, noodles, which Marco Polo brought from China, and the tomato. Immediately understood, its fruitiness becomes the base for sauces, so noodles slide.*

The potato: *First mentioned in Europe in Seville, 1539, in a monastery garden, where the vitamin-rich potato had been brought by Spanish ships. Came to Germany 1588 through Clusius. At first in botanical gardens, then because of its flowers in ornamental gardens of castles, finally in domestic gardens as additional food, until in 18th century it takes over the fields. Precondition for the population increase in 18th and 19th centuries.*

Where the noodle is, the potato isn't (see Italy, Switzerland). Unsuspected delights still need to be discovered in the potato's proletarian tuber.

It'll take days to get these cards in order again. From the next room I can hear the rhythmic squeaking of a bed. The parquet floor is shaking a little under my feet. I look at the photo of the woman: an intelligent face, she's talking, if one looks closely, not to the photographer but to someone standing next to the photographer—no, he must be sitting. This couldn't have been taken standing, the photographer would have had to stand on a chair. Also the slight inclination of the woman's posture to the left indicates a table, probably a café table. I'll ask Rosenow if he can show me a photo of Rogler.

An outline for an exhibition: *The Potato, Nourishment and Pleasure.* At the top, the names Max Rogler and Annette Bucher. I read that the astonishing propagation of this fruit (one tuber can produce thirty or more tubers) and the strength as well as vitamin content, in other words, the nutritional value, gave it the reputation of being an aphrodisiac. Whoever cultivated the potato could raise and feed more children; to the outside observer this seemed to increase the potato's potential value.

Next door the bed was squeaking louder, now I can hear the thrusting groans of a male voice, followed by quiet panting. My parquet floor joins in, swaying quietly in rhythm. I'm about to press my ear to the wall, but stop at the thought that somebody might see me standing there, idiotically hunched against the wall, listening. I lock my door. Suddenly there's a fierce knocking, metallically loud, threatening. Somewhere in the hotel or perhaps in the apartment above or below someone is hitting the heating pipes, wildly, outraged, full of hate. Next door it quiets down. The knocking stops. The idea that the couple next door might now think I'd been banging on the pipes embarrasses me a little. They seem to be taking a breather. And the floor has stopped swaying.

I pull out another card, on it typed:

> *The explorers brought the potato, corn, the bean, the tomato from America, these were the New World's wonderful gifts to the Old, truly nourishing gifts. The Old World's gifts in return: measles and pox.*

Clearly this came from an aggressive period when Rogler was still making use of Dialectic Materialism as a methodical leverage for his opinions.

The floor's vibrating again, the gasping, panting next door starts up again, and so immediately does the drumming on the heating pipes as if someone had been waiting to take out his outrage, disappointment, all the accumulated hatred of the past days and weeks on the heating pipes. The hammering must be coming from the apartment below, gets quicker as the panting gets faster as if someone were playing on a huge xylophone, and increases until at last the finale of deliverance, a man's voice crying out in release. Now the floor is firm and quiet under my feet again. The knocking on the heating pipes ends with two blows reverberating like an echo. But I can still feel a quiet quivering of the floor. I strain to hear, hold my breath, at last, the woman's high-pitched cry of pleasure. Silence. Only in the distance, from the furthest room, the sound of a saxophone. Next door laughter, then again a short, businesslike squeak from the bed. How wildly the two of them had lived it up acoustically, really uninhibited—I admired it. Not once had they let the pounding on the pipes disturb them. I'd always wanted to have some of this unembarrassed indifference to what other people heard and thought. Next door, water was running in the washbasin.

I took out my tortoise-shell cigar case and lit my last cigar, although the hotel owner didn't like people smoking cigars or pipes in the rooms. But, since in recent years I was known here as a nonsmoker, the stale smoke would be attributed to my predecessor.

I read in Rogler's bird-track script: *Revisionism? Why not, if one concentrates on vision, revidere, to look again.*

That way, when theory and reality fail to agree, one avoids concluding: So much the worse for the both of them, that being not only bad, but idiotic, namely collective delusion.
"If there were only beets and potatoes on this earth, perhaps someone would then one day say, it's a pity that plants are upside down." Lichtenberg.

This presumably is the body of thought seen by the party leadership as provocation, if not actually subversive. The suspicion that potato research served as a smoke screen for criticizing real socialism.

Poetic passages also; for example, there was a card headed: *Epilogue: White is the blossom, or red, and quickly fades—the melancholy blossom of the potato. Marie Antoinette wore it in her hair. Under the blossom hang the little red fruit capsules. They contain the sublimity of the heavens, as the tubers in the earth the power of the sun, seed of the Gods, primeval waters of the Apsu that stand snow-clad since the beginning of time, rocks plunge sheer, dampness runs black down the stone's grey, now darkened by a cloud, from white to grey, to black, clouds, and in the soil the tubers are clouds. Like the wind, like the rain, white rain, like the sun, incomparable, like the earth, heaven and earth unites, strength and water.*

I read the list of names of potatoes. Incredible, the names there were: Rogler had divided them into four categories under the headings: Potato Poetry, Potato Politics, Potato Technology, Potato Jokes: one beetlike specimen was called Dolkovski's Stella; another, full of eyes, Early Rose. Topaz, Prince's Crown, Hindenburg, Prince Bismarck indicated conservative cultivators, then there were functional names such as Woltmann Industry 34, SAS, and cranky names: First of Nassenheide, Thiele's Giant Kidney, Blue Mouse, and I found one variety with the name of Early Blue, but none called Red Tree.

I was reminded of the little lost box and of Rogler's years of effort describing the taste of different kinds of potato. How often he must have boiled and then sampled potatoes. After all, his work was based on empirical experience. And at the same time self-exploration. Or perhaps he fried them, and here whether he fried them in oil or butter would have been important because either would have changed the taste. With what words do you convey something for which there are as yet no words? The thought that this work might have been destroyed was so embarrassing, in fact so truly painful, that I got up and ran from the room to get a new bottle of beer from the hotel kitchen. I sat down, drank, and tried to distract myself by blowing a few smoke rings—first a large one, then medium size, then the small one that was meant to fly through both the others. I succeeded beautifully with the first, the others were formless little clouds and quickly came apart.

Red Tree, my mother had told me, he said it so conspiratorially, really strange. I was studying in Paris when he was taken into the hospital and at the time it never occurred to me to go to Hamburg, although he was my favorite uncle.

Red Tree. A simple misnomer, that's how I'd explained it to myself at the time, the color red put in place of the color green, as it were. A game we sometimes played with the grown-ups when we were children, shifting the meaning, so substituting table for chair, window for armchair, pot for ceiling. Lay the chair and push the window to the wall, then you'll be able to look out of the armchair. If you then also changed the verbs around, said go instead of see and paint instead of sit, verbal madness broke out; though it all still made clear sense to the speakers, their meaning dragged like a train behind what was said and mental confusion set in. Words crawled out of mouths like tortoises, driving the grown-ups from the room: Cut it out. Only this uncle listened and enjoyed himself.

Perhaps, though, something quite different was hidden behind the Red Tree. Perhaps all it meant was a street in Hamburg, the Rothenbaum Boulevard. Perhaps my uncle was only trying to remember something that had pushed its way in between this Red and the Tree, but that in dying remained inexpressible.

Red Tree.

I can't recall that this uncle ever tried teaching me any kind of lesson, that he ever yelled at me. If he went down to the harbor with me, it was more or less as equals, in a way that I'd experienced with few grown-ups. And another thing, he never spoke badly about other people, not even about my father whom he knew despised him. If anyone complained or was cross about someone who wasn't present, my uncle would say in his thoughtful way, oh well, you have to understand, and then he'd try to explain the behavior of the person being criticized. As a child one thing I knew for sure, he'd never talk badly about me. He had time to spare, which according to my father was because he did nothing, he was lazy. He really did have time, for me as well. We'd go through the old town, down to the harbor, to the Elbe. There we'd sit and watch the tugs, the ships that moved in and out, and he'd talk about his voyage to the South Seas, as a cook. These weren't spectacular stories as he never set foot on land. He learned how to blow smoke rings on board. He really could have performed in a circus. He could even blow the five Olympic rings into the room. He smoked a cheap weed and listened to stories. For example, one a stoker had told him. The stoker had been a soldier in the German Expeditionary Corps that took part in putting down the Boxer Rebellion back in 1900. In Shanghai the rebels who were taken prisoner were executed by the Chinese authorities. They stood in a long row and waited for their turn; that meant the delinquent had to kneel, stretch out his head, then the executioner struck off his head with an executioner's sword. The others then moved two paces forward. One young Chinese man stood in the queue, reading. He was reading a book and moved slowly forward without looking up. A German naval officer watching the executions asked for the reader to be pardoned. The Chinese agreed. Someone went up to the young man and told him he was pardoned. The man snapped the book shut and walked calmly away.

In the breakfast room the next morning I kept an eye out for the couple who had slept in the room next to mine. But there were only the four musicians from a jazz band from Chicago, three Blacks and a White, and they were spooning out their five-minute eggs.

I ordered a large breakfast with coffee, read the paper, but couldn't concentrate because I kept thinking about the taste catalogue. Should I phone Rosenow right now and confess I'd lost the little box? But then I said to myself, better first phone the Lost and Found. A young man came into the breakfast room, behind him a young woman, clearly the couple from the next room. The young woman was carefully made-up, only her eyes were a little swollen. They sat down, ordered breakfast, read the paper, so apart and each in a world of their own, I simply couldn't associate the night's gasping, panting, groaning, shrieking with these two people. If at least they'd held hands or exchanged languishing looks, but she handed him the butter across the table with a friendly smile, drank her coffee, carefully, so as not to smear her bright red lipstick, dabbed her mouth where, I liked to think, pleasure had after all left its mark in the dimples at the side. She gave me a short searching look and then gazed indifferently out at the sunlit balcony. And I took care to stop staring at the couple.

When I got up and was leaving the room I heard laughter behind me. I turned. They were looking at me, laughing in a friendly way, and I remembered the hideous ridges in my hair. I ran my hand thoughtfully over the back of my head. I could even feel the ridges with my fingertips.

I took a taxi to the Lost & Found Office. We were stuck in a traffic jam. Half the street was torn up and the extracted pipes and cables lay like intestines on the sidewalk.

Do you often get fares to East Berlin," I asked the driver.

"Nah," he said, "not if I can help it, don't know my whereabouts here—after all it's a foreign city—different ways, different customs. Nah, the mood is, everybody should sit pretty. Without the Wall, that's a good one! Have you heard this one: What's the difference between a Turk and an East German?"

"No."

"The Turk speaks German and works."

"I've already read that one somewhere," I said and refused to laugh obligingly.

I described the little box to the woman at the Lost &
Found Office, said "Inside there's someone's life's
work, a taste catalogue for the different varieties of
potato."

The woman looked at me suspiciously. "Potatoes?"

"Yes, there are index cards inside, cards that have
been written on, that is."

"Now just a minute, you said it was a catalogue."

"Not a catalogue in the sense of the mail order kind,
but in the original meaning, I mean, what shall I say, a
register, a list."

"What was the color of the catalogue?"

"It's a little wooden box."

"Ahha."

"So big, a light color, Biedermeier. Cherrywood."

"More of a yellow then, or red?"

"Red."

"Value?"

"Not that much from a material point of view, but
its ideal value—irreplaceable."

"One minute." She disappeared, came back, said:
"No, nothing like that here."

"What can I do?"

"Well, try putting an ad in the paper. If you do it
now, it'll be in tomorrow."

She gave me the phone number of the *Tagesspiegel*
and the *Berliner Zeitung*, one for the west city, one for
the east. She pushed a notepad over to me.

I wrote: Small Biedermeier box with potato catalogue lost in taxi. Academic work. Generous reward if
found. Then the hotel telephone number.

"You can shorten it," said the woman, "save money.
Just write: Looking for potato catalogue. Biedermeier
box. Generous reward. And leave out academic. Or no
one's going to believe there's a generous reward."

"I thanked her. As I was leaving I turned round, I
was about to give a wave, but saw she was grinning behind my back. Was it a malicious or just an amused
grin? Then yet again I remembered my jagged haircut.

At the first shop I came to where jeans, leather jackets,
and headgear were being sold, I looked for a cap, pre-
ferably without a logo, at any rate not with Rangers
on it or, in some overblown lettering, Eagles or Bulls.
But in this shop there was no cap without a sign. The
smallest was a green label with the inscription Donkeydoodle.

"Is that a sports team or a musical group?"

"Rugby team, I guess," said the salesgirl, a slim girl
in a tight black pullover.

"Good," I said, "I'll take it." One would have to
come very close to me to read the inscription. I put on
the cap with the visor towards the back. The salesgirl
looked at me for a moment, then she said: "No. If you
don't mind me saying so. You need to put the cap on

the right way round. With Donkeydoodle in front you look a good twenty years younger. I don't mean by that you're not in good shape for your age."

"Thank you," I said, turned the cap around, but pulled it low down over the back of my head so the visor pointed straight up at the ceiling, paid and left.

The Polish wedding

I'D TAKEN A TAXI THERE. THE BORDER HAD ONCE been here, the fence, the raked death strip, the concrete slab-covered walkway to passport control. The tracks were still visible in the undergrowth, now cyclists rode along the patrol lanes. Fences, mines, automated gun towers, they'd all in the meantime been removed. Two shelters and a house were still standing, all of prefabricated concrete and ruthless ugliness.

"This was a base for the border troops," the driver said, "here fox and hare say goodnight to each other now. Shall I wait? If you're not meeting anyone here it won't be so easy to find another taxi."

"Yes. Would you mind waiting a moment?" I paid and got out. There was a smell of roasting meat, a distorted tango was coming out of a loudspeaker, clearly a warped record. I went over to the low building where a large company placard promised punctual furniture moving and safe furniture storage. BERGER'S MOUNTAIN TRANSPORT MOVES MOUNTAINS. Windows and doors stood open, I signaled the taxi driver to go.

A man in a crumpled white linen suit was sitting in the office, his feet on the desk, and smoking a cigarillo. In this shabby whitewashed office with its revolving ventilator running, he seemed like a Brazilian tobacco planter. He looked up from a city map that hung open across his lap and asked, without taking his feet from the desk, "What can I do for you?"

"I'm looking for Dr. Rogler's potato archive. Formerly Academy of Science," I said.

"Hm," he said and then after a short pause: "That stuff is going into the dumpster soon."

"Why?"

"No one's paid for storage for the last three months. I'll leave it for another three months, then the gig's up."

He stood up, took a key down from a board and said: "This way."

I asked him how long he'd had this furniture warehouse.

"Since just after Reunification. I bought the complex for a song."

"Are you a management expert?"

The man, who looked like a tobacco planter, laughed: "No. First lieutenant."

"First lieutenant?"

"Yes. National People's Army. After Reunification the dream was over, time to hang up the uniform. That's when I founded the moving company. It was pretty clear that Reunification was going to set a few things in motion, old owners and new owners arriving, and those who didn't own, who rented, leaving. Logistically very interesting. Moving companies stand a good chance here. The bank immediately gave me a loan. And business is good, very good. I'm pleased with the changes, I'm my own master now. Here, these are my people, all Poles, hard working, industrious. You won't perhaps believe it, but I'm satisfied, organizing moving services is fun."

We went over to the shelters. Young people sitting and standing there, a lot of men, some women. Wooden tables, benches, a few chairs. Over a grill a suckling pig was being roasted on a spit. Three young women were sitting on a creaking blue and white Hollywood swing.

"One of my convoy drivers just got married." Berger spoke Polish with the women, he spoke it quickly without faltering. The women laughed, he laughed, jovially sent a little cloud of smoke in the direction of the young women who started to swing harder, then suddenly braked with their feet. He went up to one woman and let her draw on his cigarillo. She took a puff, choked on the smoke, coughed, and laughed. "This is the bride," Berger said.

I took off my cap, made a formal bow, and kissed her hand.

She stood up, the back of her white blouse was soaked with perspiration, there was also a damp triangle on her skirt. She fetched a glass, handed it to me, a man filled it from a bottle. "A really good vodka," said Berger. "Drink up, these two got married in Poland two days ago, now they're celebrating here with friends." They raised their glasses to me. I said: "I wish you happiness, health, and a long marriage." Berger translated for them, we clinked glasses. Down the hatch! Someone put another record on the player, again a tango. The man was already refilling my glass. Everybody here wants to clink glasses with me. I'm drinking to everyone's health. I tell them, Cheers! And now the bride's drinking the second—or is it the third glass—in one glup. She's a sturdy woman, a strawberry blond. She asks me something, they all look at me expectantly, their movements and their speech have all slowed down, dragged out like syrup on this warm, or rather hot afternoon. Have I got a wife, Berger translates. Yes. They all want me to drink to her with them. Cheers! They laugh. The tango drags, I ask myself, is it the record that's warped or my perception? No, the words are also slowly dragging their meaning behind them. Now another bottle's brought out from the icebox, the glasses filled. "You have to drink to that too," says First Lieutenant Berger. "To what?" Cheers! Do I have children? No, I lie, so as not to have to clink glasses to each one of them. I try to get rid of the schnapps glass. They want to drink a toast, may you have children. "No," I say, "not another glass, not in this heat, and besides," I say, "I haven't eaten yet," and, say I, "it's only twelve o'clock." They bombard me with words. I slowly crouch, I don't really want to do this, I want to stay upright but something is powerfully drawing me down, I'm crouching, they're all looking at me in amazement, I take this in quite clearly, it's like a group photo the way they're standing here staring at me; then I land on my rear end.

"Man," says Berger at whose feet I'm sitting, "what have you let them do to your hair? You look as if you'd fallen into the hands of an apprentice barber."

"What?"

"Yes, at the back, three lanes, I wanted to tell you earlier. You won't even know it. You don't see yourself from the back."

"I know," I say, putting the cap back on with the visor at the back. "The man who cut my hair used to mess up the entire Politburo. Routine sabotage." Berger looks at me baffled for a moment, then his face grows suspicious and he says something in Polish. The bride runs off and brings me a thick crust of bread, and a man with a tattooed two-headed eagle on his chest hands me a piece of the suckling pig that's now stopped turning and is stretching its four legs to the sky. I think to myself, I think, why is it imploring the sun. "So cold yesterday and so hot today," I say to Berger. I'm chewing, I'm sitting in the shade and chewing, chewing very slowly. "It's just occurred to me," I say, "why the dinosaurs became extinct, because the animals' masticatory muscles worked too slowly to take in sufficient starch, that's to say, turn ferns into starch. They became extinct because of their slow masticatory muscles." The Poles look at Berger, probably want to know what I'm saying. But Berger just waves his hand. I chew, and slowly the tango rhythm comes back to the right beat.

"So," says Berger.

"Can I have a glass of water? My tongue's so dry."

A Pole hands me a bottle of soda water.

"So," Berger asks again.

"I'm fine." I stood up, they all watched me, friendly, not mocking, not gloating. The floor moved a little, but I was upright.

"This way," said Berger, "I'll take you to this potato archive."

We passed some little concrete igloos. Flies swarmed here, fat, blue-black shining flies.

"What are these concrete caves for?"

"They kept the guard dogs here. This is where the kennels used to be. German shepherds for the border patrol."

Tables, armchairs, stools, chests of drawers stood stacked in the shelter, some under plastic sheets. Now and then you could hear creaking, cracking. "The wood's working," said Berger. "Originally trucks and private cars from the Territorial Army stood in the shelter." A narrow row of windows ran along the top, just under the flat saddle roof. It was hot in here, and the smell of things used over the years hung in the air.

"Here," said Berger, "this is the archive, but it's not complete. That's not because we've lost anything, but some of the boxes were collected by another moving company, they were called in by the department. Dr. Rogler gave us the contract for the rest. He made the payments for storage, on a long-term contract till two months after his death, I only learned about that later when there was nothing in the account. But no one else has shown any interest."

"Did you get to know Rogler?"

"No, I only spoke to him on the phone. Here's another one of these archives. How socialist festivities are celebrated: birthdays, weddings, GDR youth initiations, instructions for socialist party games," he pulled a card from a box and read out: "The joke, based on class. It's also not being paid for anymore, but I'll leave it, it's got its history. And you never know if it might not be needed after all. He pointed to the four boxes on which "Potato" was written in felt-tip. "If you need anything from there, take it. It's all going in the dumpster in three months' time at the latest. It'll cost another fifty then. There's nothing free in this world, not even throwing things away."

I opened a box. Books about the cultivation and processing of potatoes. In the other box: photocopies, recipes, books in Cyrillic. The potato in the Russian language. Rogler must have spoken Russian well, there were excerpts, among them comments partly in Cyrillic script, then German:

> *Potato cultivation goes hand in hand with drinking schnapps. For reasons of climate, but also mentality and history. War and Peace. The potato at Borodino? Watch fires. The reason the Irish took to potatoes so quickly, because they couldn't be trampled like the grain harvest in lunatic wars. A tuberous root has something clandestine about it.*

I pulled the plastic cover off a sofa, it was covered with a hideous poppy-red material, but it was comfortable and didn't sag. It probably belonged to a rising GDR specialist now being retrained in administration or in insurance somewhere in Düsseldorf, Hamburg, or Stuttgart, which also meant that it wouldn't do to have such realistic poppies around at home.

I read:

> *Frederick II and the potato war. Frederick didn't know dumplings, his misfortune. Also from the military point of view. Into the potatoes, out of the potatoes. Orders during autumn maneuvers. Battalion commander says, Into the potato fields: regimental commander says, Get them out!*

I put up my legs. The vodka was making reading a slow and heavy business.

> *The potato has military connotations, at least in Prussia. The peasants were ordered to culti-vate it. Old Fritz set up guards so the suspicious peasants, who didn't want to eat them (what the peasant don't know he don't eat), would steal them. Because what is guarded in Prussia has to be valuable.*

> *The peasants were ordered to. Command econ-omy, as the preparation shows. Boiled as a stomach filler. To this day, like what goes with it. The People's Own Canteens.*

Inside one book there was a yellowed fold-out chart of various types of potato, neatly drawn and hand-colored. This shows what's typical, I thought sleepily, much more clearly than a photographic likeness.

In the background in the dim light coming from above stood some oak furniture, a wardrobe, a table, chairs, then some kitchen furniture, white, varnished, a kitchen shelf above the table, next to it a tall broom cupboard. It was as if these towering pieces of furniture were moving in a wind, yes, they were bending like trees, the wood groaned, in the shade, on the ground knelt my brother, whom I only knew from war photos. He was trying to pull open a drawer, he was kneeling,

I'd forgotten that he didn't have legs. It's so hard, he said, to get at the cupboard drawers from down here. Office cupboards. I began tearing out all the drawers. They were full of paper carefully crushed into small balls. I unfolded one of these balls and saw it was pages covered in my writing. But there was one particular drawer my brother wanted opened. It was the only one that couldn't be opened, not even by force. It was stuck. I only pulled weakly, but acted as if I were pulling with all my strength. You have to want to. Let's go, said my brother.

"Shall we go," said the voice above me.

I shot up.

Berger was standing by the sofa. "Do you want to come with me? I'm driving into town now, I can take you."

Berger was standing in the shadowy hall. It had to be late afternoon, if not already evening.

"You fell asleep. That was the vodka. Did you find what you were looking for?"

"No." I shoved the Russian books back into the box, but grabbed the hand-colored chart of potato varieties and went out to the car with Berger.

Proteus rises from the sea

I DIALED THE NUMBER SPRANGER HAD GIVEN me and let it ring seven, eight times, was about to hang up when someone picked up the receiver: a scream, a crazy, piercing scream. A man was screaming as if he were being slit open. "Hello," I cried, "hello! What's the matter?" Silence. A silence coming from a larger space, then a distant, faint panting, a quiet creaking that had to be from a heavy solid object. Sighing. A sound as if a cork were being pulled out. Silence. Whispering, a woman's voice, incomprehensible however hard I tried to listen, a strange, almost childish whispering. A man's voice: "Yes, why not, turn over," a deep sigh, a lover's deep sigh, also quiet panting, gasping, a flapping sound, again, I thought, I'm being pursued again by wild raunchy panting—yesterday the people in the next room at the hotel, now two strangers interrupted by my phone call who simply picked up the receiver and probably put it down by the bed. That is, if they're not doing it on the floor. Suddenly silence. A different space, different acoustics, flat, a woman's voice: "Hello, don't hang up, you have the right number." A crackling sound, the same woman's voice again but from a different space: "Hello," and while I was hesitating, scared, should I simply hang up or say I had the wrong number, the voice again, businesslike: "Hello. Who is it?"

I didn't give my name but, something I've never done before and following a spontaneous impulse, gave another, calling myself Bloch, Dr. Bloch, said I was doing some research, but then added, thinking after that acoustic ride on the roller coaster I might be misunderstood, "it's about potatoes, I'd been given your number, your telephone number by Dr. Spranger. He said you'd worked on potatoes." Even while I was saying it I thought how idiotic it sounded: "it's about potatoes." Silence. The woman said nothing, I heard her clear her throat. "You are Mrs. Angerbach, aren't you," I asked again to be on the safe side. And as there was now an acoustic void at the other end, nothing to be heard, I called: "Hello, are you there?"

"Yes," said the woman's voice after a while. "I plagued myself with that for over a year: the potato in German postwar literature. Who gave you my number?"

"Mr. Spranger. I want to write about the potato, that's why I'm also interested in the subject of the potato in literature."

For a moment she hesitated, and I immediately recognized her trick question, "Is that monstrosity still in Spranger's room?"

"You mean the grand piano? Yes, it's still there, a black lacquered storage space."

"Good," she said. "Then we'll meet at the Greek's, Lefkos Pirgos. Neukölln. Emser Straße. The best way to get there is with the U7."

Four tables with grubby white plastic chairs stood outside the restaurant. Two tables were taken, a girl sat at one, a woman at another, too much heavy make-up, hair dyed a plastic pink, thin and matted because of the dyeing, sitting beside her on the ground a dog, a long-legged mongrel that, with its head to one side and with an astonishingly long tongue, kept taking pieces of meat from her plate. I hate unrestrained dogs, that's why in Berlin I'm always struck by the number of dogs running around, many more than in Munich. Berlin dogs are especially pushy, not hostile, if anything friendly, and seemingly trained to go for the genital region of strangers. The crazy answering machine seemed to go with the pink matted hair and the cur eating from the plate. I was about to walk away when the girl at the other table waved to me. At a first glance I would have said no older than twenty at the most, even younger, a schoolgirl perhaps, smooth childlike face, a delicate nose, white-blond hair cut short, bristly, that triggered a reflex in me to stroke it.

"Was it you who phoned me," she asked.

"Yes, how did you recognize me?"

"You look as if you're looking."

I sat down. She had a glass of wine in front of her and was calmly and nonchalantly smoking.

"Retsina," I asked. "Yes, it's the right thing in this warm weather." She crossed her legs, bare suntanned legs that disappeared under a wide leather jacket. Her skirt must have been extremely short as there was no hem in sight. She noticed my glance. And as if by chance, but still in response to my look, she pulled down the zipper on her leather jacket. Two delicate nipples stood out under the T-shirt. On the T-shirt a red star, the Soviet star with a T on it.

"Tupamaros," I asked, "the urban guerillas?"

She laughed and said: "You're still from the good old days. No, it means: Texaco. Your generation sees political signs everywhere, even if it's only a gas pump. I know that from my father," she said. She jiggled her foot a little—it was in a canvas tennis shoe, leaned back in the plastic chair and flung back her leather jacket. One of those jackets cut exactly in the style of an American bomber jacket, the sort you can buy for a high price on West Broadway. Sewn-on pockets, a small dark red leather strip, above it the squadron number. On a round leather patch, an eagle punched in silver plunges, claws out to strike. The skirt was just a narrow black bit of stuff.

"Is that a genuine leather jacket?"

"Yes, why?"

"I just wondered."

The Greek came, and she said: "One shepherd's salad," and then turning to me: "I can recommend it. And the retsina."

"Thanks," I said, "but I'd rather have a plain salad." At the same time I was annoyed I'd let myself in for the retsina which I didn't like, just to put this girl, who on a closer look was really a young woman, in a receptive mood.

"We can get out again, open the windows. Air the place out," said the Greek. A self-adhesive border with a meandering pattern surrounded the windows. He went to the other table where the plastic pink woman was sitting and asked if she'd enjoyed the lamb. The dog licked its chops, the woman nodded.

"You're researching potatoes?"

"Mr. Spranger told me about your work. And did you use Rogler's archive?"

"Yes. He was still alive then."

"What sort of a person was he, this Rogler?"

"Nice, even very nice. Helpful and friendly and decidedly witty, he had a surreal humor. For example, when he told about the potato beetles the Americans allegedly dropped onto the GDR, well, in the fifties, and how a party secretary in Brandenburg literally always tracked the pilots from West Berlin with binoculars so he could report the invasion of the potato beetles. The way he imitated it, that stiff-necked stare. He had a real gift for pantomime. I'd die laughing without him even saying a word, just because he was imitating someone. He was quite a character, in fact, my type."

"How old was Rogler when you got to know him?"

"Around the early fifties. He could easily have been my father. But I've a weakness for older men. They're just more interesting." She looked at me and I forced myself not to look at her legs again.

"And Rogler put his work at your disposal?"

"Yes, immediately. I told him I was working on the subject of the potato in literature after '45 for my Master's, he instantly started remembering all kinds of things. After all, he'd been collecting everything to do with potatoes for years. He'd worked through literature looking for the potato as subject and classified it under headings like cultivation, recipes, picture images, sayings. The thickest peasants have the biggest potatoes. The potato as a literary subject. The potato in Hermann Kant, in Strittmatter, Bobrowski, Christa Wolf. Unfortunately Rogler's index was rather one-sidedly geared to East German literature, at any rate it figured more there than with the Swiss authors Max Frisch or Friedrich Dürrenmatt, where there was hardly anything."

She took a sip of retsina, lit a cigarette, and carefully blew the smoke past my face, but I still smelled it and I thought, this is her breath. I myself would have liked a cigar now, but the day had been so hectic I hadn't managed to buy any. And again I smelled her breath. The sun was setting. In the sky distant clouds like feathers, slightly orange at their western edge. Above us in the tree, a linden tree, a blackbird was singing. On the house wall someone had written "NAZIS piss off." The SS in runic letters. A few houses away a Turk was standing outside his fruit-and-vegetable store wiping an apple with a cloth, calmly polishing apple after apple. He'd already turned a light on in his store, it brightly lit his hands. "Potato fires and clouds like sacks of potatoes in Günter Grass, potato salad in Uwe Johnson, I enjoyed the research. But the writing was terrible."

"Could it be," I said, "that potatoes don't appear in any other literature as frequently as in the German?"

"Could be," she said, "except perhaps in the Irish. Something for comparative literature. At the time I wanted to go on working for my Master's, but I didn't get a grant and I couldn't find a job. There are so many German specialists, like sand in the ocean. The same happened with me as with Rogler. He'd already been fired. He struggled through on a research contract, but it was limited, two years, an academic foam-rubber mattress to soften the fall a little, after that he would have had to drive a taxi. But then suddenly he was dead. Heart attack. I was at the funeral. I howled like a dog. A woman spoke at the funeral, but she wasn't a minister. Rogler was an atheist."

The Greek came and brought two shepherd's salads.

"I really only wanted a simple salad," I said.

"Oh," said the Greek, and suddenly he spoke a very faulty German: "Ohkay. Shepherd salad good. Can take back." But he made no move to take the plate away again.

"Leave it then, I'll eat the salad," I said and tried to put on a friendly face.

The young woman looked me over first, then smiled at me, then at the Greek, her teeth sparkling as if lacquered. She put out the cigarette she'd just lit and started eating. The Greek collected from the plastic pink woman who got up and left with her dog.

"Do you like the salad," the young woman asked.

"Yes. Or rather, to tell the truth, no. I don't like these shepherd salads. Greek cooking leaves me cold. I know, with the heat, then all these cold things are quite pleasant, but I still wonder why any Italian salad with the same ingredients tastes better than the Greek, they almost always taste like fodder from a silo—mixed with some rancid goat's cheese."

First she looked at me surprised, then a small straight, hostile fold appeared between her eyes. "I don't think so at all. How can a person generalize like that?"

"No, of course not. At night all cats are grey, says Hegel, he's not saying here that black cats are invisible, so they can't be grey."

"Well," she said, "I like Greek food, I think it tastes totally good. Besides, from the tone of your voice I assumed you also liked it."

"No, unfortunately not. The tone of voice deceives."

"They're simple dishes, and they taste like the landscape from which they come."

We sat for a moment in silence, she smoked, I looked at the street where a few children were still playing hopscotch in the fading light. The Greek briefly appeared at the door, looked over at our table, but, as we didn't order anything and no other guests had come, went back in, switched on the outside lantern, a soft golden-brown light.

"Do you often go to Greece?"

"Yeah. In the last few years I've been to Crete," she said, "always for the olive harvest. I rent a scooter and drive across the island to a farmer I help with the harvest. During the day I knock the olives down from the trees with a pole. The olives fall into nets set up under the trees. At night I sleep in a little house built from fieldstone. The windows are open. Cicadas shriek—yes, you'd have to say they shriek. Sometimes, quite suddenly, they're quiet, that always shakes me up. There's no electric light. Only a kerosene lamp. I lie on my bed and read. Guess what I read?"

"D. H. Lawrence."

"No, the *Odyssey*. I've read it three times on Crete. One of my favorite parts is where Proteus comes out of the sea and lies down next to his seals."

While I was trying to stuff the slithery iceberg lettuce leaves into my mouth, she declaimed: "Now around him gather seals and sleep; children they/of that wondrous woman, the sea./From the grey flood they rise/snorting the bitter smells of the salty deep."

I said, "They're very nice, those bitter smells of the deep," and pushed the rancid-tasting olives to the edge of my plate. "If you don't mind my asking, when I phoned you there was something on the tape. It was, how can I put it, a little unusual."

"My answering machine. One could make a social study. Some people record the *Trout Quintet*, others Cole Porter as a signature tune, others explain yet again the purpose of the machine: this little machine serves to keep your message for me—these are the novices. And then there are those who say in an imploring voice: Don't hang up, speak after the tone! I'll phone back immediately. Those are the lonely."

"Yes," I said, "and that's just it, your text had a radio play quality."

"Thanks. It's something like my company logo. What the silver shaving tray once was for barbers, my transmission is for me. But it wasn't switched on properly when you phoned. It's usually on my business number. A special rate incidentally," she said, uncrossed her legs and crossed them the other way. There was a light pressure mark on her thigh, it slowly colored brown again. "It's my job. I don't make a secret of it."

"Of what?"

"Well," she said, "I earn my money by telling stories." She looked at me: "Get my drift?"

"No."

"I earn my money by telephone sex. Chill out would be more accurate. Yes. Everybody gives me a funny look at first. But I enjoy it and the money's right. Totally clean, no touching, and you can and have to react spontaneously. Not in that stupid way most of them do: Now, my boy, jerk off. I'm here too, right here, my hand's down here, right here, between my legs: gasp, gasp, gasp. Plain embarrassing, it's for aural illiterates. No, I let anecdotes develop, possibilities, like in one's head, like reading. Studying helped me here. Telling stories is totally erotic. Secret desires take wing. Unlike women, most men are voyeurs. After all, the eye is the organ of distance. With the ear, things go straight into the brain, and pictures are registered. It just takes more fantasy."

She uncrossed her legs again, then crossed them the other way. Again that light pressure mark on her thigh, and then I suddenly noticed the fine blond down stand up on her legs, fine goose pimples covered her thighs as if she were freezing. She'd noticed my look, my gaze, and when I looked at her, caught out, a tiny smile flitted across her face, a friendly smile but mocking too. I felt I was blushing, a feeling I hadn't had for years. I tried to cover my unease with a laugh: "Are you cold?"

"Just a little shiver. It'll pass."

"Couldn't you tell me one of your stories?"

"No, I can't do that, I really can't," and she raised her hands dramatically as if she wanted to fend off an indecent advance. "Even the thought of sitting opposite you while I'm talking is embarrassing, no, I need the phone, something in-between, I can't see the other person, that's what releases my imagination, but like this, here, in front of you, no, that would be quite impossible. Don't you want the olives?"

"No."

She picked up an olive with her fingertips and put it in her mouth.

"Incidentally," she said, "salad in postwar literature is almost nonexistent. People eat all kinds of things, bockwurst, bratwurst, curry sausage, soup, above all soup, but significantly no salad. The unhealthy nutrition of the fifties, the sixties, Günter Grass aside, is also documented in literature. Probably all the Kristleins, Weberbecks, Jacobs were pimply." She laughed, said: "They looked like the people coming over now from the former socialist countries. I can recognize them instantly despite the Boss and Armani suits, their complexions still give them away."

I forbad myself to look at her brown legs, tried to concentrate exclusively on the oversized lettuce leaf I was trying to cut up with my fork. "The spread," I said, "at least as far as the tomato is concerned, is from the south to the north. Unlike the potato, which spread from the north to the south. My mother for example, who was a very good cook, never used olive oil. And with tomatoes it was something similar, at most they sometimes came on bread, in slices, but never in a salad, at any rate not in my home. Instead she made an incomparable potato salad with homemade mayonnaise. But naturally it depends on the potatoes, they have to have a taste that isn't too much an individual taste, and definitely not of turnip or moldy carrot but that delicate nutty taste that has to blend with the mayonnaise, a little secret."

"But," she said, "of course that's a ton of calories."

"Indeed, I'm sure you also know the potato was considered an aphrodisiac. A botanist in Nuremberg in the year 1634 writes that he had potatoes baked for him and, having eaten his meal, suddenly ran after his cook." She laughed, and I shot a quick glance at her legs. She blew smoke softly past me, but even so I could still smell it. Her mouth smelled the same.

"Did you read the story about the tomato–eater in Rogler's notes?"

"No, good God, I'd never have finished. My job was to compare literary quotations."

"Well, in 1840 in Salem, New Jersey, Robert Gibson Johnson astounded his fellow citizens by eating a tomato before their very eyes. At that time people still believed you had to cook tomatoes for at least three hours in order to draw out the poison. It was an historic act on Johnson's part. A scene as if written for Gary Cooper: the man sits on the steps of the town hall and cool as a cucumber eats the diabolical fruit, a tomato, that was still ribbed then, it would only become round through cultivation later. How Grace, the banker's daughter, fell in love with him, left her betrothed—a rich rancher—to have this courageous tomato-eater father sixteen children by her, thereby visibly proving the libido-enhancing properties of this fruit to his fellow citizens. He was the inventor of ketchup, which he extracted from the mysterious red fruit: the golden apple, paradise fruit, love apple."

I couldn't help it, I had to look once more at the delicate, slightly lighter inner side of her thigh after she crossed her legs again.

She stood up, with a quick tug pulled down her tight black ribbed skirt, sat down again. "Potatoes and sex, you'll only find that in Grass, hardly anywhere else," she said, visibly aiming for a more matter-of-fact tone. "I like the story about the tomato-eater," she said. "I'll keep it in mind. If it's okay with you."

"Sure, it's from Rogler's archive anyway."

"It's exactly the kind of thing that helps me with my present job. There are plenty of anecdotes, I collect them: Claudius who sang the praise of the potato, and Klopstock who enjoyed watching women gathering potatoes, he raved about rounded buttocks. People talked about my stories. My clients include politicians, male and female, and many arts graduates, for example, who studied German literature, women too by the way who've worked on the visualization of texts, in other words literary barbiturates. They're really hot on the phone, no visualization, what they want are juicy stories, just what they normally forbid themselves. Hands above the blanket! They're the ones who are always afraid of having fun that's beneath their standards. They're madly serious. Mostly from lower-middle-class families. I know it from myself, spiritual heights through depth. It took a while for me to see what utter rubbish that is. My profession helped. I record the conversations. Perhaps I'll publish them someday: relationships with oneself and masturbation. It would make a few people look pretty silly. What you heard today, that voice, I mean the scream, he's one of those. A totally inhibited type, I know him from the university. But on the phone, anonymous, or so he thinks, out come screams of masochistic pleasure. You have to hold the receiver away from your ear. The other's also a recording. I recorded my husband when we were in bed together. Recorder next to the bed. I played it back to him later. Of course I asked him and he didn't object. He's just told me today when he phoned me, he always listens to it, he's taped it from the phone."

"If it's not an imposition, I'd like to hear one of your stories over the phone."

She looks at me. Her iris is light blue and this only brings out the dark of the pupil more strongly. I take my glass and act as if I'm gazing intensely at the rest of the honey-colored wine, but look at her legs which she's just draped the other way round again: blond down, delicate goose pimples to the hem of her skirt, tiny light dots cover her brown thighs.

She looks at me, laughs: "Shivering again, but I don't mind." She zips up her black leather jacket and the Texaco T-shirt disappears under it. On her kneecap, which stands out so delicately, there's a scar, narrow, light, a good three centimeters long. On a sudden impulse I touch the scar with my fingertip, she starts lightly, and I quickly ask her in an emphatically matter-of-fact tone: "How did you hurt yourself?"

"Oh," she says, "when I was a child I fell on a curbstone. Nothing dramatic." She puts the pack of cigarettes in her pocket. "I'm cold. Let's pay. I'll give you my business number, I'll make an exception. I usually never give it to people I know. Call me. Tonight. It's a crazy day."

"Why so?"

"It's the longest day of the year." She looks at me: "And the shortest night. Everybody's acting crazy today. And most of them don't even know why. They blame the change in the weather. No. The baker this morning said he'd fallen asleep by the oven. He showed me the burned rolls, a whole basketful. The Turkish tailor who does alterations, downstairs where I live, usually a totally calm guy, suddenly yells like a gorilla. Completely blows his top. I race down. There's his daughter out on the street, she's taken off her chador and says: I got a boyfriend, a German, a Protestant vicar. I'm moving out. The father yells his head off. Doesn't do any good. The girl calmly walks away, the chador over her arm. Just before this my husband phoned me, he wants to move back in. Totally out of his mind. We were together four years. I left him over a year ago. We were friends, and today on the phone suddenly he's crying. In four years I never heard him cry once. He said don't record this, please. I'd already recorded it, so I erased it. And then later wished I hadn't. He cried so quietly, very restrained, soulful, it made me instantly think of a line by Benn. Never lonelier. Or is that Stefan George? But I said: No. Four years we were together. Then suddenly it simply didn't work, in bed. And a friend of mine left her husband too after four years, already once before that she'd also left a man after four years. The four-year cycle. And then my friend told me she's read that there's a hormone that produces this four-year cycle. It sees to it that for four years there's erotic tension, turns you on to your partner. Strictly speaking, the time it takes to conceive a child, to have it, to breast-feed it, then to wean it. It's a hormone that looks for closeness—that means fidelity—that regularly produces sexual attraction, but then stops being produced, at any rate not for the partner, it simply stops. What happens then, sex, first you have to convince yourself to do it, then force yourself if you can't just lean back and let it happen."

"I always thought," I said, "it was because we'd stopped growing in the other's eyes, that is, we lose all our potential. Then there's only attraction where something grows, as trees do, and the prerequisite for that, as botanists know, is a chaotic state of affairs. Once things are in order there's no growth, so no mystery either."

"Exactly," she said. "This hormone simply stops growth, that's how you need to look at it. Suddenly it's gone, kaput, no desire and also no more hassle."

"Why not write about your experiences?"

"No, no inclination. Writing my Master's was enough torture. And then, to write at length what's so easy to just talk about, no. But, as I said, I collect voices. I record them. Incredible, the desires that surface, whispered or yelled, the things people imagine. All I do is help people express them, they should, they need to be told it's a kind of sexual confession, not what someone's done but what they'd like to do, the lovely murky desires, the exciting dark corners of the imagination lit up. That turns me on. That's why I'm a success. Not just to say: Now jerk off. But to help that person's fantasy take the plunge. They need someone who'll lead them. Read the ads in *Tip* or *Zitty,* under the heading Hard. Of course, there are some that like it soft, but in a quite special way. The whole crazy business is all here—here." She tapped her temple, then mine, with her fingertips, lightly, the brush of a wing, "This is where it is. I'll give you my number. By the way, my name's Tina."

Fear of depths

IT WAS SHORTLY AFTER EIGHT IN THE EVENING when I got back to the hotel. There are no phones in the rooms, if you want to make a call you have to do it from the lounge.

On the subway I'd still tried to convince myself this phone call could be embarrassing, if only because the conversation could be overheard in the rooms next to the lounge. But even as I decided not to call I already knew I would phone. I told myself this was a unique opportunity to hear just how telephone sex worked. An experience I might also be able to use one day in my writing. But most of all I thought of the fine soft blond hairs a shiver had sent delicately on end. I pushed the chair close to the wall so as little as possible of the conversation would be heard outside and dialed, the number began with a 1–900. It only rang twice. An announcement: this call is charged at a special rate. Then her voice: "Hello, is it you?"

"Yes," I said, "I mean if you mean me, we ate at the Greek's."

"Of course I mean you. I've been waiting for your call, as you can tell, since I've turned off my acoustic trademark. Are you sitting comfortably?"

"It'll do."

"Can't you just lie down on your bed?"

"No, in this hotel the only phone is in the breakfast room."

"Shame," she said, the sibilant thrust soft as a tongue in my ear. "From my bed I can see the radio tower, the way it's lit up it looks like a very miniature version of the Eiffel Tower in Paris."

"Yes," I said, "perhaps when lit up at night and if you're lying in bed, but during the day it seems more like something out of a child's erector set to me. After all, it makes a difference whether you built a tower to send out radio waves or to fulfill a dream."

"What dream?"

"Eiffel wanted to sit in a bath and look out over Paris."

"Do you know what surprised me when I saw you?"

"No."

"That weird haircut. Those ridges, they don't really suit you, they look really queer."

I laughed, but what came out sounded stifled, more like a sob.

"Yes," she said, "that's really good, honestly," then she added, "Can't you take the phone to your room?"

"No, unfortunately not, the line's too short."

"Can you talk freely?"

"Well, not really," I said quietly, "the walls are pretty thin here."

"Too bad," she said. "I wanted to talk real openly with you. I must tell you: I was already quite curious about you when you first called. I like your voice. You see, voices are very important to me, you know, for someone to interest me they're the most important thing, I don't mean just intellectual interest, but physical. I don't even need to see the person, the voice goes in my ear and then, at any rate with me, if I like it it really goes right through me, obviously it also depends on what's being said. But the most important thing is the tone, the melody. Sometimes a doctor calls me, a consultant, an anatomist, he told me there are these two tiny muscles in the ear. For a long time no one really understood their function, until it was established that they amplified the nuances of tone, by contracting. A sound penetrates you and these muscles open and close, they increase the pleasure, since then I know why I like to listen, at any rate when voices have a certain tone, it gives me such a tingling sensation, it totally goes right through me, like your voice. You've a quiet melody and the vowels sound right."

"Really?"

"Yeah, you speak with a sounding board, really sexy. The way you ask something, the way you reply: it's way out. I thought, this has to be a man who knows what he

wants but who can still be very considerate, very tender." There was a long pause, so I felt obliged to say
something: "Well, yes, in principle, how can I put
it"—I was looking for something to distance me, an
ironic turn of phrase, but then I noticed the numbers,
numbers that were downright spinning in the little
white machine standing next to the phone and register-
ing the units. The person before me had phoned for
twelve units. Normally when I phoned Munich at
night the machine rolled the numbers slowly, they
crawled like tortoises one after the other and each one
carried off sixty pennies. Now they were racing like
an electricity meter when all the electric fixtures in a
house are on. I stared speechless at the numbers.
"Hello," she said, "can you hear me? What are you
doing now?"

"Me, why," I said, "nothing."

"You should know that from your voice I thought
you were much younger."

"Yes," I said, "that sometimes happens to me." I
think to myself, you couldn't have replied more idiotically. "Idiotic," I said.

"What?"

"Well, what I've just said, I meant to say I'm quite
content to be the age I am. It's not a problem for me.
Perhaps that'll change in a few years, I'll feel nostalgia,
possibly envy when I see young men."

"Oh," she said, "that's how all of you always imagine it, that the younger men are better at it"—she paused for a moment—"which happens to be true."

"Is that so?"

"Frequency decreases with age, but something else improves."

"But what?" I asked and was annoyed with myself at the lasciviously furtive tone of my question which I quickly made sound as if my interest were theoretical: "Sex, at least where feelings are concerned, is one of the few areas that aren't public, we still exclude others and we're excluded, precisely because in this depart- ment behavior is quite individual, there's the reason for our eager, unrestrained curiosity."

"I know," she said, "it's how I make my living. I'd like to be completely honest with you. The strange thing is," she said, "I personally don't find men really attractive until they're over forty-five. There's a simple reason, I get totally sexy when I can turn them on so that they suddenly have that surge of hormones, the adrenaline rises. That's the secret of erotic power. Suc- cess and an exciting life are a turn-on. That's why most older men have a way with younger women. Men have to be older, at any rate with me. The twenty-year-olds talk about how they're planning their careers or about the mischief they got up to when they were boys. Older men simply have more to tell you, two, three marriages, kids from hell, disaster and success in business. Of course it all depends on what's said and in what tone of voice. You know, when you asked if I was cold, that was something else, that's when I saw the way you were looking at my legs, it made me shiver, totally good, like now if I think about it, it's going right through me."

I stared at the numbers which, if I was seeing them correctly as they whizzed by, had raced up from the initial 12 to 180.

"Are you listening?"

"Yes."

"Did you know an older man was to blame for my marriage breaking up."

"No."

"Yes. I married at twenty-two. It lasted exactly four years, those famous four. Then it happened."

"What?"

"It's a story"—she hesitated—"a little like with us. Are you listening to me?"

"Yes, I'm all ears."

"That's how it should be. Well, it began because I wanted to do something about my fear of depths. The fact is, I can only swim where I can stand. And paddling around in the non-swimmers pool is always embarrassing. It was when I was doing my Master's. It was a terrible time. I had insomnia, I had headaches, migraine attacks, I felt as if I was being skinned from the neck up. Yes. Even the ends of my hair hurt, I didn't dare touch them. When I brushed my hair I'd feel a raging pain tearing all the way into the base of my skull, yes, right in my head where words take shape, talking hurt, so did reading, and writing certainly did. My arm, my right arm was so heavy, so stiff, I could hardly lift it, and my back was full of tension, completely in knots. It was as if I were paralyzed. I read my notes, references, quotations, I felt like I was drowning in all the details. Terrible. I went to a doctor recommended by a friend who also suffered from migraine. In a quiet friendly way he asked me about my love life, and I said there wasn't one at the moment. My husband was very considerate and didn't pressure me. The doctor made me describe the pain in my head, how and where exactly it began, he examined me and then he said: Swimming relaxes, a good swim, an hour, then you'll be able to sleep at night. It was winter. So, an indoor pool. And that's when I said to him: I can't swim, I'm afraid of depths. Then there's only one thing for it, said he, three times a week to the pool, first in the shallow end. Widths, swim across and back, and then slowly week by week work your way to the deeper end. I was a little disappointed. I'd hoped for some medication that would simply take away the pain. And now I was supposed to go and swim. But then I did go to an indoor pool. I went in the morning four times a week and swam. It did me good, I made slightly better progress with my work just like I was slowly working my way past the non-swimmers marker, but it took a while before I finally let go of the rope marking the division. Sometimes I held tightly onto it

to catch my breath, and I'd enviously watch a man who
swam there every morning like I did, but you should
have seen him, how he did the crawl in complete control up and down the lane, did his catapult turns, you
could see how exact and precise his movements were,
right down to his little finger. Sometimes he'd hoist
himself up onto the edge of the pool. The amazing
thing was, he was already an older man, mid–fifties, hair
streaked with grey. But he had a fantastic body, no pot
belly, not even the first signs. Muscular, toned, fantastic. One day we collided, instantly my confidence collapsed, I began flailing frantically, kicking in all directions, felt I was slipping sideways into a void, then I felt
his hand on my stomach and that calming, reassuring
voice, like yours: You've had a scare, he held me, I
floated. He swam with me to the edge of the pool. We
sat there a moment. I told him about my fear of depths,
the shock, and how it had suddenly come back."

I stared at the numbers that were getting near the
300 mark, and I wondered what I should tell the hotel
owner tomorrow—a long distance call to Tokyo or a
business call to San Francisco.

"He told me you had to concentrate on the movements, that's to say completely on yourself, observe
what you're doing, arms and legs, are they stretched,
stretch your arms, legs right into your toes, and most
important of all concentrate on your breathing, that's
the secret, he said, and you'll lose all your fear of

depths. So next time we swam side by side, sometimes he held me for a moment, corrected the way I held my head, my position, and then once his hand slipped down and that's how he held me, for a moment he held my crotch, he gave me a frightened look and took his hand away again. I'd seen the man three times, sat with him at the edge of the pool: he was an architect, married, had children. As we sat there, our feet hanging in the water, he talked about building projects, a school, a post office somewhere in the East, a house for dual occupancy; and always with enthusiasm, even fanaticism, as if we were talking about the Eiffel Tower. And he swam with such determination, such economical movements, but strong and with very little splashing. I could hardly wait to go swimming in the mornings, looked forward to seeing him, and when he didn't show up for two weeks I paddled joylessly up and down the non-swimmer's rope, I even went on the weekend to be sure not to miss him. Then, after two weeks, he was back. A trip because of some business offer or other. I told him swimming on my own wasn't fun, and he said he couldn't have waited any longer, and then after swimming we went to the changing cabins, and that's where it happened."

There was silence at the other end of the line. "What," I said, "that's where what happened?" She seemed to be drinking something.

"I'm drinking a glass of red wine. Can't we clink glasses, shall we, over the phone."

I said, "There's no red wine here, only beer in the refrigerator, I'd have to go to the kitchen first."

"My God," she said, "that's very Spartan." At first I wanted to contradict her and ask if she thought mini-bars had more atmosphere—then I saw the numbers had moved up to 578.

"What happened," I asked.

"I slipped. He held me tight. Very tight. I felt his wet body, felt mine, I shivered though the pool was warm. I wanted to pull off my bathing cap, couldn't really get a grip on it, my hands were shaking. So, gently he pulled the cap from my head, and suddenly we kissed, or rather, we lunged at each other. What did I taste, I tasted chlorine, a smell I don't really like, but amazingly at that moment it was a really raunchy smell—crazy, no—the smell came from his wet, naked body while outside sleet was coming down, suddenly children were shrieking, a school class had come for swimming lessons. We pushed open a cabin door, locked ourselves in, stumbled against the wall, without saying a word he took, no, he tore my bathing suit off my body. Wait," she said, "I'm getting a cigarette."

I heard a crackling sound, she'd clearly put the receiver down on the table, then footsteps growing fainter, a metallic pecking. Could she be wearing stiletto heels on a parquet floor? At any rate she was no longer wearing tennis shoes. Was she still planning to go out tonight? To meet a man? I tried imagining her in a black dress. But then my eyes again fell on the little white machine in front of me, on the black meter with the little white numbers that were still evenly and tirelessly turning as I listened to the silence at the other end of the line, they now clocked 590 and would soon exceed 600. I added up and it already came to the crazy sum of 360 marks. I was angry, yes, I felt my temper rising, and thought, should I go on letting her make a fool of me or simply hang up. On the other hand, I said to myself, it would be really absurd not to hear the end of the story when it had already cost so much. And of course I wanted to see her again. Then I heard the pecking of the heels, from a distance, it came closer, a rustling sound. "Hello," she said, "sorry," she said, "I had to pee. You must give me your address, then I'll send you a copy of my work. Of course it's very much from a literary historian's point of view."

I'd made up my mind to say to her right out: Girl, get on with it. But now I wondered what address to give her since I'd given her a false name. "Best to send it care of a friend," I said and gave her Kubin's address.

"Just a moment," she said, "I'm writing."

"So," I said, decidedly impatient, "what happened next?"

"No," she said, "you have to have a little patience."

"Time is money," I said.

"True." She laughed. "We were in the changing cabin. Of course even then the word was on my mind: AIDS, but crazily, against my better judgment, I didn't care. Not at all. It was narrow, that cabin, walls everywhere, wire netting above, a bench on which I knelt with one knee, my body, my head turned to the corner of the cabin. When I gave a loud sigh he pressed his towel in my mouth, I bit into it, silenced, but every one of my suppressed screams reverberated in me all the louder. They all lunged up into my head, in my body, the way I was muted and gritting back the screams in silence until everything inside just flamed up, until it all throbbed and then suddenly collapsed, then a soft, a fulfilled shudder of pleasure. It wasn't until he carefully set me on my feet, then I noticed my legs were wobbly, my knees were shaking. I could hardly stand, I had to brace myself against the wall. Somebody pulled at the cabin door. We heard children yelling outside. I quickly put on my bathing suit. We listened. The children's shrieks grew fainter, we raced out of the cabin, he first, looking to right and left like after a bank robbery, then me. I changed and saw I'd put the bathing suit on the wrong way round, the label on the outside. I drove home. I wasn't embarrassed, that even surprised me, it was my first affair on the side, as people say."

And again I heard her take a sip. "I'd always imagined a bad conscience would weigh me down, tear me apart, that I'd reproach myself in despair—not at all. Whenever I thought about it it made me laugh, I laughed right out loud. It had been fantastic. But I was a little unsure what I'd do when I saw my husband, how I would act towards him in the evening."

There was someone at the hotel door, unlocking it. "Just a moment," I said. A hotel guest came in, a young man, he was carrying his racing bike on his shoulders. He glanced at me in the lounge, saw me phoning, said: "Good evening. Good evening." He went squeaking on down the parquet along the corridor to his room.

"Who was that," she asked.

"A young man from the hotel with his racing bike."

"I always take my bike into the house," she said. "The days when you could leave it chained outside are over. Now they even saw through those huge locks, they quickly freeze them and bam, they're cut through, just like that."

"You were telling me about your husband after, well, after what happened at the pool."

"Yes, in the evening my husband came, I'll call him Thomas. I went up to him, not tense, not bottled-up inside, quite open, I even had the hots for him, yes, and thats when I hadn't enjoyed it with him for months. I think if I'd met the man somewhere in some house, in a room full of furniture, a bed, chairs, a wardrobe, private things, it would all have related to his life and mine. But this way it was like in another world. And I think that's why what people call side affairs happen in hotels. An anonymous place with its standard decor that's quite unlike how we live at home. When I thought of the pool it was, how should I put it, as if I'd seen it all in a movie. Myself included. Can you understand that?"

I glanced at the counter which was now nearing 700 and said, "Yes, of course, but what happened then?"

"It didn't bother me that the other man, that's what I'll call him, the other man was with his wife, it was like another world, similar, I thought, to how I was with Thomas. Every week we'd see each other at least twice. We'd swim for a good half-hour, then we'd shower, warm, hot, quickly go down a row of cabins and when no one was watching dash into one where we'd fall on each other, never lying down, there wasn't room you know, but in every possible position. For instance, there were two coat hooks in the cabin onto which I could hold tight," she laughed, and I heard her take another sip. "Positions like you know them from reproductions of Indian temples, the craziest ones, not just the normal ones when you're making love lying down. And always in that crazy silence because in the next cabin someone unlocks the door, a coat hanger scratches, a quiet cough, while I had to take care my head didn't keep banging against the partition wall. I'd be screaming inside, gasping, breathless, struggling for air, both of us red in the face, scratch marks on his back, his chest. God, I whispered, what have I done. I pointed to the

two red streaks. What will your wife say? I've told her I
go to play water polo twice a week, he said."

I laughed.

"You can laugh, so did we. We burst out laughing in
the cabin. When we came out of the cabin a man was
standing there staring at us, at me. It gave me a terrible
shock, the man seemed somehow familiar, I spent the
whole day wondering where I'd seen him before."

"And," I said to bring her back to the subject, "did
your husband notice anything?"

"No. He asked me once why I cut my nails so short,
as short as you do with children who bite their nails.
The chlorine is making my nails brittle, I said, they're
splitting. And of course he wanted to know what had
got into me. I didn't turn away from him, on the contrary, he said, I was different, quite a different person,
more free, it's like you just cut loose. That's from swimming, he said, I'd lost my fear of depths. You're letting
yourself go. You're really wild, he said, even wilder than
when we first got to know each other. But I think really
he'd only forgotten what it had been like then. A good
two months passed that way. I slept like a log. My
headaches, the tension had disappeared. I was making
progress with my work. In fact, everything was just fantastic. Wait a minute, I want to fill my glass again."

I heard splashing, then the sound of swallowing.
I suddenly suspected I was hearing fabricated background effects. I'd like to have said, I don't give a damn

about your work problems. "Listen," I said, "are you recording this?"

"No, I'm not doing that with you."

"So, you saw each other twice a week?"

"Yes. We met twice a week at the pool. We were better at it now, it wasn't such a strain to hold my breath, to hold in the screams. We had got into practice, you could say. I had time to enjoy his skin, it was wonderfully soft, fine, despite the chlorinated water. Then one day, after we'd come out of the cabin and were sitting at the edge of the pool, he said: The one thing I really long for is to stretch out beside you, to hear you close to my ear. To lie next to you a while. And something else—quiet. Quiet around us. He suggested meeting for a weekend."

I saw the counter leap from 852 to 853 to 854.

"But how did it happen, I mean, how did your marriage end?"

"Don't rush me. We've time. So I said to Thomas, I want to go to Frankfurt over the weekend to see an exhibition, a school friend lived there, I hadn't seen her in years. I didn't want to spend the night at her place, I said, because I didn't like her husband. I lied to Thomas, in all those months it was the first time I'd needed to lie. Until then I'd simply gone swimming in the morning. I lied with indescribable revulsion, it struck me as something especially nasty, something I really don't like to think about, that moment when I said: I want to go to an exhibition. Sure, sounds nice, said Thomas. I left on Friday afternoon, we met in an anonymous but expensive hotel. He'd booked separate rooms so as not to raise any suspicion if one of us got a call from a spouse. He'd thought of everything."

I heard her take another sip, there was a pause.

"And what was it like?"

"A disaster." She took another sip. "Too bad you're not drinking something too."

"Yes, a shame—but why a disaster?"

"I could see the bathroom mirror in the mirror in the room, and him in front of it, the way he brushed his teeth, very nicely, red white, red white, can you imagine, I was lying there waiting and he's cleaning his teeth like in some educational film against cavities, and then he even uses dental floss. We'd had steak. Then he came and said, listen, are you using contraception? Of course not, I lied and said it was a bit strange he was asking me now. It was a fiasco, it was stupid. And it didn't come off, as people so nicely put it. It was ridiculous. I slept in the other hotel room. We traveled back separately to Berlin. I had plenty of time to think while the Intercity drove on the replaced GDR track. Also about my marriage."

The meter now had gone over the 900 mark and I was intrigued about what would happen when another zero, for which there wasn't a space, was added. Would everything jump back to zero, or would the machine fall apart? I'd been on the phone for almost six hundred marks, the most expensive phone call of my life. And of course I couldn't tell this to anyone. "Well, tell me," I urged.

"I opened the door and, as he came up to me, told Thomas everything. He was so astonished, he just sat there and listened. No despair, no reproaches. That same evening I moved in with a girlfriend. I never saw the man again. My husband and I were good friends, we had an understanding until today when he phoned and played crazy. A totally crazy day. And now you've crossed my path. You know what, I feel like swimming. Without any fear of depths. If you want, we could meet at a pool. Would you like to? Hello."

I stared spellbound at the meter now approaching 1000. The 7 came, the 8, then the decisive 9, the counter jumped back to 0.

"What are you doing? Are you doing something to yourself?"

"No. Nothing, I was thinking."

"Would you like to?"

"Yes," I said.

"We'll need to hurry," she said. "The pool is open until ten."

"I don't have swimming trunks."

"You can rent them there. Take a cab. See you soon."

I hung up, the figure was exactly 13, so one unit

more than before. I wrote 1001 units under my room number and wondered how I was going to explain this tomorrow. I quickly pushed aside as shabby the thought of writing down only one unit. For a moment I still tried to persuade myself simply to stay in my room, not to go to the pool; you can't allow yourself to act like this, I told myself, but then again, you have to see the pool just for professional reasons because this is a story that could be developed. And of course I wanted to see what she looked like in a bathing suit and I wanted to get an idea of the cabin size, she'd be sure to show it to me. I took a hotel towel and ran down to the taxi stand.

I really was able to rent trunks at the pool. It was one of those old colorfully-tiled pools that were built in the Wilhelmine period. It smelled of chlorine and toe-fungus medication, and it was extremely warm. I began sweating. My glasses misted over. I left them in the cabin. I'm not very shortsighted, but enough so as not to be certain that I'd recognize her at a distance among the other swimmers, especially if she wore a bathing cap. I showered as required, went to the pool, took a dive that—fully stretched—was quite elegant, did a crawl down one lane, warm, the water was exception-ally warm, in fact unpleasantly so, did a catapult turn, did the crawl back, but by now hugely out of breath, until I swam into an elderly woman who gasped for air and complained but I couldn't understand her. I'd swal-lowed water and coughed till the tears came, I kept my-

self afloat treading water, it tasted disgustingly of chlorine. I looked around. Only old people, old men, old
women bobbing awkwardly up and down. It was as if an
old people's home was on an outing. At the edge of the
pool there was a blond boy hanging from a swimming
pole, the strap around his body, doing aquatic exercises
supervised by a swimming instructor. I'd never imagined swimming lessons were still being given according
to such an old-fashioned method. I swam up and down
in that piss-warm water for another half an hour, quite
effortlessly. Now and then I propped myself up on the
edge of the pool and looked around, there was no sign
of her. I was by far the youngest person there. A loudspeaker said, please leave the pool, the baths are closing
in fifteen minutes. I went to the cabin and dressed.
It was only as I was leaving that I saw the notice:
SPECIALLY HEATED TODAY. SENIOR CITIZENS
EVENING.

A glass of buttermilk

A KNOCK WOKE ME. SOMEONE WAS KNOCKING ON the door of my room: Telephone for you! I jumped out of bed, quickly pulled on a sweatshirt, slipped on my slippers, and went to the lounge where some of the hotel guests were already having breakfast. The receiver was lying on the small telephone table. "Hello," I said and heard a deep male voice, but couldn't understand a thing. It was a moment before I recognized individual words: "Potato. Catalogue. Varieties. Tastagooood. You loookin?"

"Yes," I said, "I'm looking for a catalogue, a taste catalogue of various kinds of potatoes."

"Tastagooood," said the voice with a jovial laugh.

"Do you have the little box," I asked.

"Haveallkindabutitgonnacost."

"Yes, of course. Where can I meet you?"

"Hilton Hotel, Gendarmmarkt, in lobby, four?"

"Ok," I said, "Hilton Hotel, four o'clock and please come with the taste catalogue."

"Gooood—butyounixbargainpricegonnabegoood."

"Of course there's a reward for finding it."

This voice laughed from depths that gave it a booming heartiness. A spontaneous, sympathetic laugh, I thought.

I hung up. So the little box had turned up again. I was so relieved I must have let out a happy gasp or perhaps even said something, at any rate when I turned, all eyes were on me, a woman was holding a roll she'd bitten into in front of her mouth as if she'd forgotten about it, she'd stopped chewing, a man looked at me with a stupid stare. I said good morning, turned around, and immediately whispering started behind me. I went back to my room.

It wouldn't be easy for people to make sense of what they'd heard over their breakfast eggs: potatoes, taste catalogue, potato varieties, reward for the finder, and on top of that my terrible convict's haircut. It's not every day you meet a sales representative for potatoes in a hotel where one would expect Stockhausen or Anselm Kiefer to show up. I decided I'd go to a barber this very day and have my hair cut properly. Presumably the driver had given the little box to one of his Russian acquaintances who was now coming forward as the finder and the two would split fifty-fifty. I didn't care as long as that shitty taxi driver didn't show up personally.

I shaved. My eyes were still slightly red from the chlorine. Idiot, I said aloud to my reflection. I'd hoped for some extraordinary story full of riotous perversions,

and instead—the story of an affair on the side I could
have thought up just as well for myself though not, I
had to admit, so that I showed up in the story. In the
mirror I saw myself shaking my head. Six hundred
marks that joke had cost. Crazy. I showered, put on a
polo shirt and trousers, took my jacket, and when there
was a moment's silence in the corridor, left the room,
locked the door, and tried to leave the hotel without
being seen. At that moment the young woman who pre-
pares the breakfast came from the lounge.

"Hello! Did you sleep well," she asked with a cheerfulness that immediately gave me a bad conscience.

"Yes."

"It must have been pretty noisy here last night."

"I didn't hear anything."

"After the concert the musicians from the USA carried on playing late into the night, until morning. A
wild night. An extra concert. I found the saxophonist in
the kitchen this morning asleep on the floor, next to the
dog."

"A pity," I said, "I'd have liked to hear it."

"By the way, you made a mistake when you wrote
down the phone units. You only had one unit but you
put down a thousand and one." She laughed.

"No," I said, "that's correct."

"A thousand units? That can't be, we don't even
have that many in a month."

"Yes, well, there's a reason."

"My God, where did you phone?"

"Australia. A friend works there, in Alice Springs. He's an ethnologist."

I looked at her; she didn't believe me, and the way I'd said it, so embarrassed and awkwardly I wouldn't have believed it either. "I had to phone him," I said with emphatic cheerfulness. "His wife's left him, and he's stuck out there with the aborigines who can't understand his problem. They want to clink beer cans with him because his wife's finally left for distant Germany."

"Oh," she said, "that's weird. Would you like a small or a big breakfast?"

"Thank you, nothing today, friends have invited me for breakfast," I lied. I wanted to get out of there as quickly as possible, didn't want to have to assure her one more time that the one thousand and one units were bound to be right.

I passed the phone booth from which I'd tried to call Tina back last night. I'd made up my mind to say to her what she'd done to me had really been worth six hundred marks, and then to give a cool laugh. But her phone had been constantly busy, and that's when I began to get really angry, an anger that kept growing, because, I said to myself, now she's on the phone with someone else, perhaps she's telling a more exciting

story, and again the meter you normally don't even notice is running, so that later you're astonished at the
high telephone bill. She'd probably been phoning, in
other words, earning money, while I was swimming
lengths at the pool. And now there was another randy
fool having stories told to him. When I thought of the
word fool I immediately thought, that's you, and said
aloud: Yes, you fool, you're an idiot, a complete idiot,
you're an ass. And I was surprised I'd said you and
not I. I'm the ass. I'm the idiot. Later lying in bed I
couldn't get to sleep because I was busy thinking how to
pay her back.

I went down a side street where yesterday I'd seen a
small grocery store. They sold bread rolls with cheese
and sausage. The store bell rings. An old woman in a
white overall was serving and a younger one, who could
be her daughter, was helping her. "I'll have a roll, a roll
with cheese."

"What kind of cheese would you like? Emmenthal,
Gouda, Tilsit?"

"Tilsit, please."

The woman's daughter cut a roll open. "In the old
days," said the old woman, "we got butter and cheese
straight from Tilsit, that was before the war. The
cheese is still called that, but the town doesn't exist any
more."

"Yes it does," I said, "it's just that it has a different name."

"No," said the old woman, "once the name is lost the town doesn't exist. There are stones left, but nobody who lives there calls the town by that name. They all speak Russian now. It's a different town. You can still eat the cheese though, it's the only thing to remember the town by."

The daughter buttered the roll and cut two slices of cheese and put them on it.

The daughter gave the woman the roll and she gave it to me. The daughter—I figured she was in her sixties—looked briefly at me, a fleeting, chilly look. The old woman gave a friendly smile, handed me the roll over the counter.

"Are there any more bread rolls," the old woman asked her daughter. The daughter shook her head. "Then fetch another ten, no, make it eight. It's nearly ten o'clock. There won't be many still wanting rolls." The daughter left the shop in her white coverall to the light ringing of the store bell. "Would you like something to drink," the old woman asks me.

"Yes, if you have coffee."

"We're not allowed to serve coffee, but maybe you'd like a glass of milk or buttermilk?"

"Yes, buttermilk, please."

She gave me a large glass of buttermilk, with it a straw. "At the end of the year we're retiring. We opened the store sixty year ago, my husband and I. He's been dead twenty years now. Business is bad. A shame," she said. "Even though it's so much easier for people to quickly buy some butter here, fresh when you need it, than running to the supermarket three times a week and then carrying heavy bags home. Are you here on a visit?"

For a moment I hesitated, shouldn't I just say yes and avoid more questions. But why tell lies to this old woman of all people, so I told her the reason for my visit.

She laughed, said, "The things people do, writing about potatoes."

"Do you also sell potatoes?"

"Yes, but only three kinds now, one waxy and two floury. We used to have twenty kinds, we got them straight from the farmers."

"Do you know a type of potato called Red Tree?"

"Red Tree, no. Strange name. But when I was a child there were names like Reich's Chancellor, Prince's Crown, and Blue Kidney. We have several hundred-weight in the cellar, they came straight from the farmers. Four heaps, next to them—coal. There was a partition wall behind the heaps of potatoes, a girl hid there during the war. When the parents were rounded up they left the girl with a neighbor and she brought her to us because we had this cellar under the store. And then we were able to feed an extra person, you see, because there was always a little extra though we had to reckon with the ration coupons. The girl's parents were very refined people. The father had a little factory, he made tuning forks for pianos there. The girl had one of these tuning forks in her bag, one of those little leather bags you used to put sandwiches in for schoolchildren. That child sat in that cellar for two years. And sometimes at night down there the girl would be hitting something with her tuning fork, ping it went, ping. You could hear it real clear at night. She did it because she was afraid of the dark. And we were afraid other people in the house would hear it. She sat in that little space until the Russians came, two years she spent sitting behind that wooden partition. When the Russians came in '45 the women hid in the cellar. The Russians dragged out the ones sitting behind the coal—but they didn't climb over the potatoes. Those escaped. But as for the others, after that," she falters, "after that the girl was dumb, never said another word."

She turned and took the buttermilk. "More buttermilk?"

"Yes, please, it's really good."

The bell rang as a young man came into the store.

"Hello," said the old woman, "yogurt culture again?"

The young man pulled the Walkman plugs from his ears.

"Yogurt as usual," the old woman asked again.

"Yes, and two bananas, as ripe as possible, please."

It was the same young man who'd come into the hotel with a racing bike on his shoulders last night while I was phoning. Tall, gangling, mid-twenties, hair with bleached strands that fell over his forehead.

"And could I have fifty grams of linseed and a ring of dried figs?"

"Just a moment," said the woman, "I have to fetch those." She went to the room behind the store.

"Hello," the young man said to me, "you're staying at the hotel, too. I saw you last night when you were phoning."

"Yes."

"I never have breakfast in the hotel," he said, "or it gets too expensive."

"Have you been there long?"

"Almost a month now. A research project. And you're working on the spud?"

"How do you know that?"

"From the hotel. It's not a secret, is it?"

"No."

"I also heard that you phoned for one thousand units yesterday. A love affair, the young woman told me."

"Yes," I said, "a crazy business." And I was about to add, to explain: my friend Ted who's doing field work near Alice Springs, when the young man said: "We can get that back."

"How?"

He untied his small Bali-woven backpack, put in both bananas and the cup of yogurt. "The magic begins with microchips, only the cultural pessimists haven't understood that yet. Phone me in three hours at the institute. This is my phone number there." He took out a little red card. "Then I'll give you a number, I'll have to apply for it first. The number will only be valid for today. Then you make the call. It's quite far away, don't let that put you off. That call will then be credited to the phone from which you're speaking."

"But how? And where does the money come from?"

He laughed. "That's the dirty trick, you've got to zap onto somebody else's line, you must know somebody who owes you something. Of course you can also phone some institution, the tax office for example. You have to keep talking until you've run up six hundred again. But the number's only valid for today." He laughed. "An open sesame for a day."

"I don't believe it."

"You should."

"But how does it work?"

"You need to ask the clever boys at Telecom. It's the so-called boomerang call. You throw the boomerang, it makes a nice circle, and you catch it again. After all, you were calling Australia, not your girlfriend."

The old woman came from the backroom with a little pointed bag.

I hesitated a moment. So the young woman at the

hotel hadn't believed my story and simply turned it round. What harm could it do, I thought, everything's already so confused, and I said: "Yes. Are you a communications specialist?"

"Used to be," he said and pushed the little bag into the backpack without untieing it again, "I wrote programs, now I'm in linguistics." He paid. "I'm doing research into the difference between East and West Berlin dialects. I need to stay with it. Things here change at an incredible speed."

"He's already interviewed me," said the woman, "I can speak High German, Berlin dialect, and East Prussian. Because I'm not a real Berliner, I'm from East Prussia, Pillkallen. That's where men and horses drink, the saying goes: only in Pillkallen the horses stay sober."

"I don't know any city where you get into conversation as quickly as here," I said. "You ask for a street name and people give you a biography."

"Yes. It was even easier before Reunification, it's starting to get more difficult now. I've got this theory," he said, "that there's an inclination in the Berlin dialect towards the use of the dative case with personal pronouns. It's a grammatical alleviation of communication. The natives of Berlin say: done gone and nicked you's head. Through the use of the dative case, the formal form of address is simply avoided. It breaks down the barriers of unfamiliarity, real slick, that dative case."

"Are you a Berliner?"

"No, I'm American. New York, but my mother's German, but from Hamburg. Now Kennedy could never have said I am a Hamburger." He looked at his watch, said, "Oh God, I have to go. I have to be at an interview. With an Ossie, an engineer, he immigrated from Saxony twenty years ago, a so-called Eastern Zone bum. Phone me. Bye."

From the store window the old woman and I watched him get onto his bike and take off, swaying and standing on the pedals. He disappeared in a sharp turn around the corner.

The old woman smiled and said: "He's always racing around. A good-looking young man, and always so nice and friendly. The things people do," she said, "your own grandmother wouldn't believe it, I mean the things he's studying. And you, what gave you the idea about potatoes?"

I told her about my uncle.

"Ah," the old woman said, "I saw someone like that once on TV in that *Bet You Can't* show. People are amazing." The daughter returned, to the sound of the door bell, holding a paper bag with rolls. "Did your uncle ever live in Berlin?"

"No, not as far as I know. He hardly traveled. He was once in the South Seas."

"Oh," said the woman, "that must have been lovely."

"But he didn't see much. He was a cook and had to stay on board when the ship came to a port because he'd signed on illegally. He went around the world once, but he could only see the beaches, the palms, the ports, the people from the ship."

"Perhaps," she said, "that spared him a lot of disappointment."

"Yes, perhaps."

"Did you like the rolls?"

"Very much."

"And the buttermilk?"

"That too. I hadn't drunk any for a long time. I used to drink a lot when my mother was still alive. Whenever I visited her she'd buy buttermilk. It makes you big and strong, she used to say. By then I was already over forty."

The old woman laughed.

"So long as one of your parents is still alive you'll always be a child."

"Well, I'd better pay. But I've only a fifty-mark note."

"Can you put it on your expense account?"

"Theoretically, yes. But it's not worth it for a glass of buttermilk and a roll."

"I'll write out a receipt for you. You can say you were shopping for a business breakfast. If everybody paid what the state asks of us, we'd soon all be bankrupt. The tax office knows that." She wrote on a receipt pad, food and drink, gave me back the change with the receipt.

One hundred and sixty-four marks: I read cheese, bread, drinks.

"So," she laughs. "It was a big breakfast. One of those brunches. With champagne and caviar. You were talking to a potato specialist."

I laughed: "Not bad. What if I were somebody from the tax office?"

"No, I'd have seen that," she said, "good luck with your work."

"Goodbye."

It wasn't until I'd left that I noticed she'd short-changed me by ten marks. I was about to go back and tell her she'd made a mistake, but then I thought perhaps she hadn't made a mistake, that this was the price for the friendly conversation and the receipt.

I went on my way and then crossed over to the Kurfürstendamm, in search of a tobacconist. Still morning, it was so hot now I took off my jacket and hung it over my shoulders. And I took off my cap. I didn't care what people thought. On Uhlanstraße I found a tobacconist and asked for Havanas, Cohiba. The salesman led me to the air-conditioned display case sealed by a glass door. I wondered whether to take four Coronas Especial or five of the somewhat smaller Exquisitos which fit into my cigar case. I smelled them and decided for the honey-colored Exquisitos. A hundred and twenty-five marks, a mighty price. My potato article was getting more and more expensive. The salesman who expertly cut the cigars for me told me that in Cuba young women, who had to be under nineteen, rolled Cohiba cigars on their thighs, it was this contact with skin that caused the fermentation in the tobacco that produced the finest aroma when smoking. In Cuba in the Laquito cigar factory I'd seen mostly older workers, though these women all sang. I didn't contradict the salesman, but put the cigars in my case, paid, and resolved to quit smoking, perhaps when this potato story was finished.

I called Rosenow from a phone booth. He answered while on the way somewhere, probably from his car.

"Did you get the things," he immediately asked.

"Yes, what was stored in the apartment. But the taste catalogue is missing."

"What? Why? It has to be in the little box."

"Yes. It's very embarrassing, but the little wooden box with the catalogue was left behind in a taxi."

I heard Rosenow's astonished quiet "No," and then another, a little louder, indignant: "No."

"Yes, I'm sorry, but in the meantime I've already tracked down the box with the catalogue. I'll have it again this afternoon."

"Look," Rosenow said, and there was an unusually sharp tone to his voice, "that little box belongs to me, it doesn't belong to Rogler. It's an heirloom, you see. I just put Rogler's index cards in it. How could such a thing happen?"

Sweat was running down my forehead. "I had an argument with a taxi driver. One of those taxi-driving creeps. He threw the big box, the documents onto the street. Then he drove off with the little box. The taxi wasn't registered. I've been to the Lost and Found Office. Nothing there. I've put an ad in the *Berliner Zeitung* and the *Tagesspiegel.* And the person who's found it contacted me today."

"Then you were lucky."

"Yes. Of course I'm paying a reward."

"Good," said Rosenow, "because it isn't just any old box."

"I know, Biedermeier, cherrywood."

"Not just that, it means something quite special to me, quite apart from Rogler's life's work inside it."

"I know. It was really unforgivable."

"Perhaps," said Rosenow, "Bucher had a copy. She must have some of Rogler's papers lying around."

"Who actually is Bucher?"

"An ethnologist with whom Rogler wanted to set up the exhibition in the West after Reunification. I'm just coming up to a red light, then I'll find the number for you." There was silence except for quiet sounds of driving.

It was hot in the phone booth. I was sweating, also because I was upset, and I wasn't sure I wanted to meet any more potato experts. I'd have preferred to quit the whole business. I pushed the door open with my foot and searched for my pen in my jacket pocket. Rosenow gave me the number. "Perhaps Bucher has a copy." And then, after a pause: "Call me as soon as you have the box. Did Spranger say anything?"

"No. But that barber, that Kramer, gave me a lousy haircut."

"Oh God, probably a razor cut, People's Army style," Rosenow's voice had that friendly, obliging tone again.

"No," I said, "more like punk, but only at the back, with plenty of ridges."

"I should have warned you. I've a good, a very good barber, perhaps he can do a repair job. I'll give you the number. You'll need to make an appointment. Ask for Puk. He really is a magician, and he tells great stories as well. Well, call me when you have the box. Then I'll come by for it."

I hung up. Wiped the sweat from my eyebrows. An embarrassing conversation, I was surprised at Rosenow's reaction, the extent of his agitation. Naturally the loss of the box was annoying, especially if it was an heirloom. On the other hand, it had lain around for months in his old apartment without him missing it. And then to become so uncontrollably upset, as if there were God knows what in the box. But probably the box was only a pretext, he was actually afraid that because of him Rogler's taste catalogue had been lost. I found the thought of this so painful I kept deliberately repressing it.

I dialed the barber's number and asked when I could come. "Just a moment. I'll look at our schedule," said a voice. "When would you like to come?" "As soon as possible, and I'd like Mr. Puk to cut my hair, if that's possible."

"We're fully booked for the time being, until July eighth, that's when there's the Love Parade. We can't manage anything before then."

"That's a shame, a real shame. Dr. Rosenow recommended you. I've been given a terrible haircut, it looks as if I've had an accident."

"Oh dear, an emergency." And then after a short pause the voice said: "All right, come around noon today, I'll try and fit you in somewhere."

I dialed Mrs. Bucher's number. A man's voice answered: "Bucher." I briefly explained my request. "Yes," he said, "come right now."

I hung up. Wiped my forehead and hung my cap over the phone so it was clearly visible. It would soon find an admirer.

On the street I flagged down a taxi and had him drive me to Dahlem. Perhaps that strikingly beautiful woman whose photo I'd found in Rogler's archives was waiting for me there.

The ring

THE VILLA, A FLASHY BUILDING FROM THE twenties, had been converted and divided into two separate apartments; Bucher, a man around fifty, lived in the upper one which had two roof terraces. He stood at the door of the apartment, in blue shorts, a faded blue sweatshirt, on his bare feet brown leather slippers. The living room was in a radiant white. The walls bare except for one picture. Red, penetrated, actually smashed open, by a blue sphere. "A Lebedev," said Bucher when he saw me gazing at the picture. It was the same picture I'd seen the day before on Spranger's wall.

"Do you know it from reproductions?"

"It's very beautiful, if one can describe it like that."

"Is it genuine?"

"Yes. I bought it on the advice of a Russian art historian. Come, we'll sit on the terrace. A large well-planted terrace with rosebushes and three little stunted pine trees. Two deck chairs, white garden chairs, a round table, open over it a huge orange sunshade. The remains of a lavish breakfast were on the table: jam, cheese, sausage, ham, it was laid for two, a bottle of champagne in an ice bucket. I had to make an effort not to immediately ask him about his wife. Steps led up to a second, somewhat smaller terrace from which a bougainvillea shone purple. For a moment I thought I saw a dark figure against the bright blue sky.

"Have you already had breakfast," Bucher asked.

"Yes, thank you."

"A breakfast glass of Laurent-Perrier perhaps?"

"No, thanks. But if you have some orange juice."

He poured me a glass. "I've already put the two boxes out for you." He pointed in the direction of a wooden deck chair." You can sit there and look through the papers at your leisure."

I went to the deck chair. A little brass plate was screwed to the armrest: TITANIC.

"The day before yesterday I saw a replica of Napoleon's camp bed, now this deck chair."

"No," said Bucher, "that's no replica, it's the real thing. I bought it in Halifax. That's where everything that was fished out of the sea after the Titanic sank was unloaded: bodies, empty life jackets, and also these wooden deck chairs. Even then they fetched a high price. I bought the last one from a Newfoundland fisherman whose grandfather had gotten ahold of about thirty of them and bought himself a new schooner for what they fetched."

I leafed through the files, the index cards, and saw right away that they were photocopies of what I'd already looked through at the furniture warehouse. Though the books were missing here.

A file with photocopies of statistics and various essays on potato diseases, land distribution, on price increases, on the weekly potato consumption of a laborer's family in 1883, in the middle of all this a photo. A man with greyish blond hair, a finely shaped nose and a moustache that hung heavily over his upper lip. The light blue, clear eyes were striking. Immediately I thought, this has to be Rogler. And the photo of the woman in Rogler's box really then was of Bucher's wife. Possibly the relationship wasn't just about preparing an exhibition, as Spranger believed. The man in the photo had on a sweatshirt that was visibly worn, but to deduce from that that he came from the Eastern Zone struck me as being a little too smart. A mathematician from Princeton or Cambridge could just as well have worn it. I leafed through photocopies that showed Inca clay jugs in the shape of potatoes. Potatoes with human heads or human heads with potato bodies, vulvas, penises— erect, limp. The folder was labeled: *The Potato. Fertility and the Art of Pottery*. A movement, a noise made me look up; on the upper terrace stood a woman in a dark dress, a black kerchief on her head. She glanced down at me. For a moment I thought it was Bucher's wife, then I saw the dark brown face. I raised my hand in greeting. The figure stood still, gave no sign she'd noticed my greeting, then looked in another direction, stepped back, and disappeared behind the blossoms.

"Well," Bucher asked, "is that of interest to you?"

"Yes."

"You do understand that I can't hand over these papers without first asking my wife. But I could photocopy for you what you need."

"Thank you," I said. I wondered, given the way he's just said this, whether his wife was actually in the house. But perhaps she was just taking a bath after the lavish breakfast. "Did you know Rogler?"

"Yes, I had the experience on a couple of occasions."

"Is that him?" I showed Bucher the photograph.

"Yes. Where did you get the photo?"

"It was here among the notes."

Bucher took the photograph. "Yes, that's him all right. Or rather, was him. The man in the moon. I'm a physicist, so my perspective's a little narrow perhaps, but what Rogler was doing had nothing to do with science. An agronomist who looked to cultural history, in other words to a rather soft science. I don't in any way want to belittle this. He knew what he was doing and really collected just about whatever there was. You should have seen him, just after the Wall came down, when he traveled to the USA. He'd been invited by some provincial university, my wife arranged it. That

was my first experience of him. Annette and I took him
to the airport. He was traveling with a friend, a botanist
dragging a huge box. The pair of them looked like
Turkish guest-workers going back home. There was a
Russian computer in the box, a computer Noah would
have rejected as out-of-date when he boarded the Ark.
The botanist was pushing the computer on a luggage
trolley, Rogler holding it up at the side. And the two
were nearly not allowed to enter the country in New
York because the American customs officials thought it
was a Soviet decoding machine. It took a while for them
to realize it was a Russian laptop. Rogler himself told
the story very nicely. He had a good sense of humor and
could be subtly ironic about himself, the way he told it
and snorted with his moustache, like that seal on television—Annette and I laughed till our sides ached. I
wanted to give Rogler a notebook, but he didn't want it,
he stayed with his index cards. Incidentally, he came
back completely changed from that trip. He raved about
New York, he'd worked his way there from a college in
Montana. His dream: a job at New York University,
though his English wasn't good enough; but he'd become really worldly, one of the first things he did was
mix us a martini, a la Paul Becker, academic, poet, and
famous mixer of cocktails in Greenwich Village." For a
moment Bucher stared into space.

I hesitated about asking him, but then did ask and
quite casually: "Isn't your wife here?"

"No." And then, perhaps because he saw my disappointment or just to avoid more questions, he said, "she's not in Berlin. I'll fix us a drink, a Paul Becker martini. The recipe is the best thing Rogler left behind. I found this potato business just too pathetic, too much interpretation, opinion, and there's always something sloppy about opinions. No, that wasn't for me. You absolutely have to try this martini."

"It's hot," I said, "I already had to drink several vodkas yesterday at midday at a Polish wedding. I must tell you I never drink in the middle of the day and, even in the evenings, at most a beer, a glass of wine."

"But you have to try this drink, beautifully chilled and very dry, just the thing for a hot day like this, even if it is still a little early. If only so that we can drink to Rogler."

"Do you think I could see a photograph of your wife? When you become so intensely involved in someone's work, you're curious to see what they look like."

Bucher went to the living room and brought me a silver-framed photo. It really was the woman whose photo I'd found in Rogler's box. So they both had photographs of each other hidden in their papers, in fact, among the charts of potato varieties. In the photograph here the woman was laughing. A charming, enticingly beautiful woman. But all I said was, yes, and thank you, and wanted to give the photo back to him.

Bucher pointed to a glass table: "You can put the

photo there." He'd gone to the black wooden Art Deco bar, opened it, and was doing something with bottles and a shaker while explaining the mix through the open terrace window. "My wife and I called it Rogler's Dream. So, very good gin, Bombay or House of Lords is best, then white vermouth. For the gin to be really dry it should be poured over ice in a shaker, just a dash of vermouth on top—Vanderbilt's butler, from whom the recipe comes, is supposed to have said, only a whisper of vermouth on top—then stir, never shake. Pour into chilled glasses, add a small piece of lemon rind."

I caught a glimpse on the upper terrace of the dark scarf covering a woman's head, probably a cleaning woman, Turkish or Moroccan; many of them had recently come illegally to Berlin to work. But this woman was unusually tall and there was something special about the way she moved, calmly, really dignified. Perhaps she was Bucher's lover.

Bucher came, saw me looking at the upper terrace, but only shook his head without saying anything. He handed me the glass, an Art Nouveau glass in a silver calyx. "Your health—Well?"

"Tastes quite fabulous."

"Yes," he said. "But it wasn't this magical drink, at least not in my opinion, that unleashed all the craziness."

"What craziness?"

"Yes. I gave up everything, profession, wife. Yes,"

he said again and for a moment distractedly pulled at his short blue trousers. "My wife is an art historian, not an ethnologist. Rosenow misunderstood that, and that in fact is where the story begins, because if she had been an ethnologist, then probably the whole thing wouldn't have happened the way it did. Because, you see, she would have known that some gesture or comment of no consequence to us could have an unsuspected meaning in another culture. In the last few years she'd been on three trips to the Sahara. Always in a small group. Three, four people. Desert means no boundaries, doesn't it, one wants to experience oneself without boundaries. The sky must be indescribable at night. I would have gone with her, but I didn't have the time. My company. I make, I made software for the municipality, for instance for waste disposal, for drinking water, cemeteries. I sold the company three months ago and since then I've been able to live free of worries and collect Russian Constructivists. My wife was particularly intrigued with the Constructivists. Since we split up I collect paintings, not out of revenge, but because it really pleases me. But I want to tell you about my wife's desert trip. Last year three months after the trip the phone rang. A voice said: Annette, please. Nothing more. My wife goes to the phone. Hangs up and says: Strange. Someone wants to collect a photograph. He's at the airport waiting. I drove out with her. It was January and bitterly cold. We get to the airport and there's a

Bedouin standing there, a Tuareg, in a totally bleached dark blue galabia, standing there in the hall and shivering like a dog, though the hall was well heated. I draped my coat over the man's shoulders, and then we left and came straight here. The car, you can believe me, smelled of camel dung.

"The man, probably a kind of prince, had sold his share of camels and bought a plane ticket with the money, first-class, round-trip. So he had no problem with a visa. He'd simply done what my wife had said—if ever you come to Germany, look us up. A conventional phrase, that's all. But before that she'd taken a photograph of him. I'd seen the photo after her trip, a truly handsome man, very good looking indeed, with blue, deep blue eyes, tall, slim, and then those long blue robes. She had, as I said, taken a photo of him, after the Land Rover met up with his caravan, and he'd invited her for tea in his tent. She'd promised him the photo and said, the way one does, that he should pay her a visit. And now he was here. It was like a movie. Completely matter of course, without any great explanation such as, I thought I'd take you up on your offer, or something of that sort. We've no children and plenty of room, two guest rooms with bathroom and a small kitchen. So there was no problem having him stay. Besides, he spoke German. He spoke a strange German, German with a Russian accent. He'd learned it from a Russian aristocrat, a woman who had come with the

Black Sea fleet to Tunisia in 1918. The fleet had fought
on the side of the White Russians against the Bolshe-
viks. And the woman, as with many officers' families,
was stranded there. A ceremonial German with an old-
fashioned polite turn of phrase: Excuse me for inter-
rupting you, but would you please pass me the cruet
stand. By that he meant the saltcellar. The way he said
it, it was always strangely dignified. He wasn't in the
least obsequious. All our circle of friends came, they
wanted to see him. Or we were invited with him. Par-
ties were given for him. People fought to travel on the
subway with him or on the paternoster elevator, to
show him the polar bears in the zoo, or just to invite
him out for an ice cream cone. He went about the city
in a state of childlike astonishment and dignified curiosity. This was, moreover, after the time when people
had taken to the streets with candles to demonstrate
against xenophobia, it was simply chic to be seen with a
black man in a blue robe bleached by the Sahara sun.
All the liberals, the amiable teachers, architects, doctors
would really have liked to keep him overnight just once.
But he never wanted to go anywhere else. He only slept
at our place, he went out with us, came back with us. He
didn't drink. He just sat gazing in amazement. And
everybody wanted to be gazed at in amazement, or at
least that he should be amazed by their lawn mowers,
their yachts, their billiard tables. It lead to some real
petty jealousy. And in our lives too, many things, in fact

everything, had changed. It must be like having a child. No more of those boring evenings, those interminable Sunday afternoons. You saw things in a new way with him, somehow strange, as if everything were bathed in a new light. For instance, he could say of the Friday evening traffic in the city: The cars are crowding together tonight. Is it going to rain? When Christmas came I finally asked him, very carefully, if he didn't miss his desert, his tents. After all, he'd seen his photo. But he didn't react to my question, he stayed. Spring came, he stayed, though sometimes now he did go down to the garden. But he never went alone on the street. Annette said he'd sold all he possessed for this journey. He's without means. She reproached me, maintained I was letting him see that he should go back. It led to more and more arguments between Annette and me, they were mostly about other things that only indirectly had anything to do with him. Then he'd always solemnly get up and remove himself, not to go to his room but to the terrace. He'd sit there under the open sunshade even when it was sleeting. As a result we'd quickly stop arguing so that he wouldn't catch pneumonia outside. We never had the impression he was without means, which actually was the case. He was, as they say, living at our expense. But we had money. He accepted everything with a regal casualness. If a bourgeois loses his money, Rogler, who after all was an informed Marxist, said then he's nothing. The aristocrat stays an aristocrat, that doesn't depend on money. It's just that then he's a poor aristocrat."

"Oh, Rogler," I said, "of course Rogler," and I remembered again why I was sitting here.

"Another martini?"

"Oh," I said, and I had difficulty wording my refusal. "No," but I couldn't come up with a reason quickly enough.

"The story," said Bucher, "is just long enough for two martinis." He refilled the glasses from the chilled silver shaker. "Rogler's Dream. We also drank it on Sylt, Annette and I. That was the last time we drank it. We go to the island of Sylt every year in the middle of May. And of course we wondered what was to become of our Bedouin prince while we were on holiday. We tried to explain to him what it meant, to go away on holiday. But there was no way of making him understand it. We'd gone out of our way to ask the housekeeper if she'd stay and look after him, as we had our doubts about leaving him to work the gas stove and the microwave oven on his own. He nodded, but gave no indication he'd stay. Clearly he took it for granted he was coming with us. I suggested simply leaving secretly, loading the luggage into the car early one morning and driving off. But Annette was really outraged. That's betrayal. You can't shatter such a trusting childlike nature like that."

I drank Rogler's Dream and thought how rehearsed

this all sounded. Bucher wasn't looking for turns of phrase anymore, didn't lose himself in irrelevant details, but told his story as if he'd fully prepared it for my visit—or else he'd already told it many times. But perhaps it only seemed like that to me because the martini had wiped out all the other agitating perceptions and I was now listening with steady curiosity.

"We drove off with him. I suspect that in the Middle Ages emperors traveled the way we did. Wherever we went we caused a stir. He accompanied us to highway service stations, in hotels, to friends in Hamburg, not like a servant, but like the ambassador of a faraway country, casually and with regal dignity. Until we came to Sylt, the island of Sylt with its dunes. We arrived and he was beside himself. The only time, incidentally, that he ever lost his princely calm. He saw the sand dunes and ran off. He let out strange sounds from his throat, a kind of yodeling. We waited—we'd simply stopped for a break—we parked and waited. We were worried, thought perhaps he'd run into a policeman. He wasn't carrying his passport or anything and his residence permit had long since expired. Annette was already imagining him being held for deportation. Then we thought he might have gone in the water, out of curiosity, perhaps he'd already been struck down by the first breaker and drowned. After all, he didn't know the sea. Couldn't swim. Besides, it was still cold, even when the sun was shining. After three hours Annette was completely out of her mind, wanted to drive off and give the alarm to send out a search helicopter, and suddenly here he was. His robe was wet, so he really had waded into the water. I have to admit, I'd dearly have liked to see him when he saw the sea, the waves, the spray of the surf, and marched in. Later he'd run down to the beach in his blue bathing trunks quite unconcerned. Before that we'd only seen him fully dressed. He'd go to the beach and lie in the sand in the ebbing, still icy waves, like one of those old women you sometimes see in Italy who never learned to swim, he'd shriek and laugh and dig his fingers hard into the sand when the spray came. Incidentally, it was only here that I ever saw something like childish fear in his face. Sometimes he disappeared in the dunes for hours. I never thought I'd be interested in men, but whenever I saw him naked, that toned, evenly brown, muscular body, I always had a deeply irritating desire to touch the muscles that connect the arm here with the chest." He cautiously tapped my chest. "Nothing more. Eventually he stopped wearing his robe, he wore blue shorts and an old blue sweatshirt, what I'm wearing now. Neither Annette nor I asked any questions, though actually here where everybody wore bath towels wrapped round them he'd hardly have stood out in his robe. He suddenly seemed, how can I put it, closer in normal clothes.

"From then on I saw a change in Annette's behavior, now that we were on Sylt, now that we saw him on the beach and in the dunes. She'd put make-up on in the morning, which she normally never did on Sylt, at the breakfast table she'd shake her freshly-washed hair into her face, the way she'd done with me when we were getting to know each other, now she looked at him through that shining silk curtain. I'd look at her, she'd look at him. I have to admit I liked looking at him, I'd already be looking forward to seeing him in the morning. Oddly enough, her looks left me cold, if anything, if I'm honest, I was jealous when he looked at her. But he seemed, or so I had the impression, not to be reacting to her looks.

"I simply couldn't understand it, that at fifty I should start to be interested in a man, though my interest wasn't primarily sexual, it was simply the desire to be physically near him.

"And then one morning he stopped speaking to Annette. He looked past her. What's the matter, I asked him. He shook his head. What's the matter, I asked her. Nothing, she said. But she was, what shall I say— confused. On the third day she had a crying fit. She packed her suitcase. She admitted to me that on an evening when I was meeting a friend, she'd gone into his room. He'd been reserved, which she misunderstood as cultural shyness, but when she touched him, tried to kiss him, he'd shown her the door. And do you know what he said? It is not seemly. Bucher laughed. One does not betray one's host. A guest's obligation wipes out the sexual impulse—can you imagine, the last wild drive we still possess, one that beats all the others, friendship, marriage, religion, fear of AIDS, every form of political correctness, all forgotten when partners are really hot for each other. And then someone comes and sets the guest's rights and the duties of hospitality above everything else.

"So then she went to a friend in Paris. At first I wanted to close her account, but then I thought it's fine the way it is. It would only have been petty. And secretly, I had to admit, I was glad she'd left. Now and then she draws something from the account, not a lot, so things stay the way they are. She didn't even take her favorite blouses or the dresses from the twenties that she'd bought in New York.

"She phoned once. It was a calm, friendly call, almost too affectionate, we talked about bills, contracts, relatives, also about this archive of Rogler's, who was dead. She cried when I asked her if I should still keep it. I think it was like a reminder of her earlier life, these two boxes standing around here. But then she quickly controlled herself. I asked how she was. Fine, she said. The tents have been taken down. The horizon is open again. Naturally that came from him, that sentence. A crazy business that we got involved in, she said, and wanted to know how he was. Fine. That was all. She'd phoned from Paris.

"I've never allowed myself to touch him. I'm sure

he'd leave instantly. Mind you, his visa expired long ago. But he still has his first-class return ticket. He'd go back to his camels that no longer belong to him. I'd gladly offer him money, the money he spent on the ticket. But, this is crazy. I'm also afraid of that. Then everything will be the way it was before, ordinary, that means normal, all colors mixed together makes grey. Against that, his calm presence. I don't even know what he does when he's alone in his room. In the morning, if the weather's fine, he sits on the terrace and prays facing east. Our shared interest, do you know what it is?"

"No," I said, even this little word now only made its way sluggishly over my tongue and through Rogler's Dream.

"The Constructivists and classical music, that's what we share. Bach and Mozart. We often go to concerts. Though he had never heard classical music before, he has an extremely sensitive ear. If Bach is being played, he sits there as if he'd turned to stone, sometimes I nudge him because I think now he's gone forever, finally completely withdrawn into himself. Then he slowly comes out of that rigid state. I've never experienced anything like it. And then we look at the Russian Constructivists. He has no time for figurative painting and he doesn't like Picasso or the Expressionists, all he does is laugh. But you should have seen him when he saw his first Yves Klein. Pure blue. I couldn't tear him away from the painting."

"And Rogler," I asked. It sounded more like Roller, the way I brought it out.

But Bucher understood. "He died quite suddenly. A heart attack. For a few months my wife continued with the plan for an exhibition, but then we separated. She left everything behind. As far as I know, there's a taste catalogue of different kinds of potato, the most important part of his work, according to Annette. But I think it's all pure fantasy."

"It's just this catalogue that I'm looking for, it's not in this box either."

Suddenly Bucher let out a strange, modulated call, a kind of yodeling, but more throaty, a call that reminded me of minarets and *A Thousand and One Nights*.

A moment later the woman appeared, came down the terrace steps, I saw blue eyes under the bleached blue head veil and the dark, regular features of a man's face. He bowed slightly and placed a brass jug on the table.

"This is Moussa," said Bucher and introduced me. "Would you like some mint tea," Bucher asked, "he's made some."

"Yes, thank you."

Bucher placed three cups on the table and the man poured the steaming tea. A kind of peppermint tea, heavily sweetened. Moussa drank and asked me what I did.

"I write."

"Are you a scribe?"

"He describes the world," said Bucher, "and people, as it were."

"Without song," the man said, "we would lose our way in the sand."

I would have tried to explain, if I hadn't found thinking, speaking so difficult, that I wasn't a singer, that he must be confusing me with someone else. But then I didn't even try, I told myself it made no difference anyway whom he mistook me for—we wouldn't see each other again.

He said, "If you would allow me a question, might I ask if you often walk or do you travel by train or perhaps in an automobile?"

"Yes," I said, "I like to travel. But I've never been to the Sahara. I've got around in Berlin quite a bit in the last few days. And I've had some strange experiences. Much more than in a whole year in Munich."

"The moon, our brother," he said, "watches over our sleep. He shows us the way. He brings rain. He leaves the dew behind on the stone. He is married to the sun, that is his misfortune. After a night with her, he wanes. Exhausted, he needs twenty-eight days to regain his strength. In three days he will fade away."

I drank the tea, cloyingly sweet and nothing like the freshness of mint.

On his left hand he was wearing a gold ring with a cameo.

"A beautiful ring," I said, "is that a roman cameo?"

He stretched out his hand, long delicately-articulated brown fingers. So that I could see better I carefully took his hand, I felt a slight shudder. He pulled the ring from his finger and handed it to me, without touching me.

"A gift."

"That's Athena," I said, "the companion of Odysseus."

He made a gesture that indicated this meant nothing to him, or that he didn't care. When I wanted to give the ring back to him he raised his hand in refusal. "A gift," he said, "the ring reveals something to you that it did not reveal to me."

I was alarmed, I wondered if, through some remark, I'd invited him to stay with me or if perhaps something I'd said, had been misunderstood. To accept this ring would mean that at some point or other I'd have to make a return gift, something he'd expect as a matter of course, possibly one of my daughters, who knows. To return it was impossible. He shook his head with a firmness that brooked no contradiction. How come, I thought, somebody would take a gold ring from his finger and give it to a guest he's seeing for the first time. I was confused, thrown off balance, and wanted to leave as quickly as possible. He accepted my thanks casually, even with indifference. Sooner or later he'll show up, I thought.

Bucher was looking at me with a mixture of envy and resentment, perhaps there was even grief in his look. Probably he'd never asked his guest about the ring's significance. And now there was nothing more to ask and Moussa would let himself be driven to the airport tomorrow.

"Don't you need any of these papers," Bucher asked. "I could send you photocopies."

"No, thanks. I don't need any. Thank you very much."

"And by the way," said Bucher, already standing on the bright landing, "your hair, what can I say, it's been hideously cut. You've three steps, or rather, ridges at the back."

"I know," I said, "thank you, thank you for Rogler's Dream."

What, I thought to myself on the way down, have I gotten involved in? To stop myself swaying, falling, I held tightly onto the banister.

Airborne

"GOOD GOD, WHO DID THAT TO YOU? YOUR wife? It's mostly wives who assault their husbands' heads."

"No," I said, "my wife gives a really good haircut, this was a barber."

"Impossible." He walked around me, looked at the back of my head, in the mirror I saw his stunned astonishment.

I last went to a professional twenty-five years ago, since then my wife has been cutting my hair, now I'm at a barber's for the second time in two days. The young man in wide black linen trousers and stone-grey T-shirt with a stylized white parachute and the imprint "Airborne" said: "Wait, before I lay a hand on you I want to fetch the boss. As a witness, if you don't mind, so no one says later I disfigured you like this." He left.

In the center of the salon—or should one say Hair Studio—the company logo outside said: Hair Design—

stood a life-size plaster replica of a statue of Apollo. I wondered if I'd offended the young man with the Airborne T-shirt by including him with barbers. I could think the words hair stylist, but I was certain I'd stammer if I said them. The young men who worked here could all have come from the *Iliad,* not an ounce of fat, athletically steeled, they cut here, dyed, washed, the tight T-shirts showed muscular upper arms or toned abs, sometimes even the navel, like the stylist next to me who was dyeing a young man's hair, fine orange streaks that he laid on over narrow tinfoil with gentle brush strokes. In the rear corner on the right, to the left as seen from the mirror, there was a small bar, in front of it a tubular steel stand: volumes of photographs, *Vogue pour l'homme,* comics; Techno music resounded out of spherical speakers, now and then the hiss of an espresso machine. A young woman in a miniscule black silk dress, probably a slip, was serving at the bar. When she bent over to the ice compartment, jacked up on her extremely high platform shoes, there appeared—as if a curtain had been raised—the twin half-moons of her buttocks. With a gentle push she shut the refrigerator door and came over to me, asked, did I want a cocktail, something soothing.

"I've already had a cocktail this morning, a martini, in fact, two. I hardly ever drink cocktails. And never during the day."

"That's too bad," the girl leaned over me to tie on

a blue wrap, I was immersed in the scent of sandalwood.

"That's too bad," she said again, "because Caribbean Dream is my speciality." By coincidence her
breast gently brushed against my right ear.

"Well all right then," I said, "I'll try one, though
my head's still full of Rogler's Dream."

"Was it good?"

"Very good, as a matter of fact."

"I wonder what you'll think of my drink."

The hair stylist next to me was working like a
painter on the young man, he dabbed his hair with a
brush, took a step back, dabbed again. Looking round,
I saw I was by far the oldest person in this atelier.

The young men in the Airborne T-shirt came back,
behind him another younger man, Butt-Head grinning
horribly on his white T-shirt. In the mirror I saw them
all now looking over at me, stylists as well as clients
were staring at me.

Both young men studied the back of my head.
"Good heavens, that's grievous bodily assault," said the
young Butt-Head stylist, obviously the boss. "You
could ask for damages. I mean it. Sue the man."

"Oh, it wouldn't do any good," I said. I couldn't exactly say it was someone working illegally, that in fact I
shouldn't even have let him cut my hair, that I'd come
by these ridges in an idiotic, almost inexplicable way.
"Anyway," I said, "it was in East Berlin."

"Not that too," said Butt-Head.

For a moment I hesitated, then I decided to say it: "The man even cut Ulbricht's hair."

"Those poor people. No wonder they had to build a wall. You were probably the victim of a revenge attack. A haircut targeting all Wessies, a kind of symbolic mutilation." The two of them, and the others, standing or sitting around, all laughed. "Your hair's been cut very well in the front, also at the sides, but at the back there are three regular ridges. Really spiteful."

"No," I said, "I don't think it was malicious. The man, he was quite elderly, just wanted to give me a fade cut."

I shouldn't have said it because the salon exploded with shrill, cackling, screaming laughter; in the mirror I looked into other mirrors, behind me, in front of me multiplied to infinity all these laughing young stylists, laughing young clients, the girl at the bar was laughing and so was the young woman at the cash register.

"I'm sorry," said the head stylist, "but it's just too funny. No, an Ossie giving a fade cut, even saying it sounds like a joke."

And they all laughed again and I did my best to laugh heartily with them. The girl came tottering over on her too-long legs and brought me the drink, Caribbean Dream, perversely colored blue and tasting of what, azure blue? Yes, there must have been something 150 proof in it because as soon as I tasted, or rather, swallowed it, everything around me grew calm, and I thought, like at the dentist when you lean back, this is the tranquilizing injection they give you to have your hair restyled. Next to me the young man was having the surplus orange dye carefully dabbed out of his hair.

"So, how'd you like it," the girl asked.

"It's good, very good."

"Are you thinking about the sea while you're drinking?"

"Hm."

"You must shut your eyes. And tell me what you see."

I shut my eyes. Again her breast lightly, softly brushed my right ear while she adjusted my wrap.

"So," she said, "what do you see when you taste it?"

"It's true," I said, "It's the sea. A beach, no, it's not a beach, it's rocks from the cliffs and blocks of concrete."

"What! Blocks of concrete?"

"Yes, probably a jetty or something like that, and the main thing. . . ."

"What," she asked impatiently.

"I can see a flag washed up on the shore, small, blue, on it a white rectangle."

"And what's that?"

"The Blue Peter."

"What Blue Peter?" I opened my eyes and looked at her, she had confusingly blue eyes.

"A flag put out at sea, it means: My nets have been caught in an obstruction."

She looked at me at a loss for a moment, then she said: "You're a fine one," and laughed. "Nicely plastered already." She threatened me coquettishly with her index finger and teetered back to the bar.

"Most people see the same thing: sand, water, and palms," said the young hair stylist with the Airborne T-shirt.

"That young woman's eyes are almost as brilliantly blue as this Caribbean Dream, I've never seen anything like it."

"Contact lenses, she's wearing contact lenses, normally her eyes are ash-can grey," said Airborne and, after a brooding look at the back of my head: "Well now, with your three dueling scars at the back of your head there are three possibilities: one—make you bald, so a shaved head. But then you'd really need to wear a gold earring."

My no was so loud, the young man with the orange-tinted hair sitting next to me shot up and the hair stylist had to quickly raise the brush so as not to dab his forehead. He gently pressed his client's head back down. "Under no circumstances a shaved head," I said.

"Okay," said Airborne, "another possibility would be—how should I put it?—make the three ridges your theme."

"What do you mean?"

"Well, I could dye them green, that would be a knockout."

"No," I said, sipping my Caribbean Dream, "no, I'm too old for that."

"Dead wrong, you can be a bit spaced out at any age."

"Yes. No. Well, not for me, if you don't mind."

I looked over at the young man who was just having the last orange streaks put in his hair. He was a good twenty years younger. And he looked over at me, but out of the corners of his eyes.

"Then there's only the last solution, but it's the simplest: I'll cut your hair very short. Those ridges will still be visible, they won't stand out so much, but they'll still be visible. And I have to tell you, then you'll look like a fraternity member."

"What? How come?"

"Well, like somebody from a school fencing club who got one on the back of his head when he was running away."

"I don't care."

"Okay, I just wanted to let you know."

What, I thought, makes this airborne man think of student fraternities, and I said: "Raise the flag! Short please."

"Shall I tint the sides a little, they're already quite grey."

"No," I said, "dyed men in their fifties are ghastly, and it gets more embarrassing every year."

"How do you think a government minister like Genscher would look if his hair were grey? A sweet old grandpa with elephant ears, who nobody would have listened to."

"No, please, just cut it short."

"Okay," he said, "first I'll wash your hair."

I had another sip of Caribbean Dream. A blissful apathy filtered through my head, which made me lean back. I saw Airborne squeeze a poison-green jelly into the palm of his hand, then he aimed the lukewarm water over my head and slowly massaged my scalp. "What made you even think of having your hair cut over there? Nobody here goes over there, except maybe to the theater."

"I was waiting for someone over there," I said, "so there it is. I'm from Munich."

"Tourist?"

"No, I'm doing research, I want to write something about the potato."

He laughed. "My favorite meal is potato skins with cottage cheese and herbs."

"Really? I once knew a girl, she liked potato skins so much she dressed up as a potato at a carnival."

He gently brushed the foam from my hair. "Don't be so uptight. You don't have to screw up your face like that. This jelly doesn't sting the eyes. I can tell it's a

long time since you had a professional haircut. You're
still sitting tensed up. Bend forward for a moment. Re-
lax totally." He pummeled my neck muscles, my left
shoulder, gently but firmly. "Here," he said, "it's really
tight." He took some jelly, massaged, "can you feel that,
a real knot, you can't run around Berlin with a knot like
that." I felt the tension I hadn't even noticed before
slowly ease. It gave me goose pimples, it was good. I
could have fallen asleep on the spot.

He gave my head a quick rub, took scissors, comb,
and began to cut with neat movements, none of that
self-important snipping in the air that Kramer had
done before my eyes, none of that threatening gesticulating with the comb.

"Didn't he show you in the hand mirror what you
looked like at the back?"

"No."

"That's all part of these old-style barbers' pride in
their profession. Never mind," he said, "it is too late to
sue, all you can do is report him. Who knows how many
people's ears he nicked out of carelessness in the GDR
days. By the way, a ring in your ear would also look
good with this short haircut. Look at Agassi. He almost
always wears an earring."

"Yes, but I'm not number one at tennis and I'm also
too old for it. I'm not making myself look ridiculous."

"But you're wearing a ring anyway, people like you
normally don't wear rings."

"True, I've only been wearing it for two hours. It was given to me. By a Tuareg. Do you like it? If you do, you can have it."

"It's quite an expensive ring I think," he said, "a cameo, isn't it?"

"Yes."

"Anyway, no thanks, I already have a steady friend. Besides, you have to be careful with rings."

"Why?"

"My friend reads a lot in the evening, and if there's something he really likes he reads it to me. I don't read much, I prefer music."

"What kind do you like?"

"Music to chill out by. The other day he read me a story about an Italian. It was about Charlemagne, when he was really old"—he hesitated a moment, then added, "I mean quite a bit older than you—he fell in love with a very young girl. All the emperor wanted was to be with this girl. The court officials became anxious. The emperor didn't concern himself with his kingdom anymore. Then the girl suddenly dies, and the court breathes a sigh of relief. But the emperor just won't part with the girl, he has her embalmed and brought to his chamber. Of course this upsets the archbishop. He suspects sorcery and orders an autopsy."

Airborne took a step back, looked at his work and said with great firmness: "No, I can't let you go like that. Those three dueling scars. It looks amateurish, no, comical, ridiculous, totally wrong. Believe me, if I do three green streaks, it'll have a magic effect."

I drank the rest of my Caribbean Dream. I thought about it, perhaps it really would be better, I said to myself, to turn these three fault lines into something purposeful, something stylish. Besides, I've had the same haircut for twenty-five years, short and combed a little to the front to hide the bald patches at the temples. Now they're exposed and, if anything, I think I look younger.

Airborne looked at me and I thought, he's taking you for a timid middle-class conformist. "Okay," I said.

He began fiddling around with bottles, poured tinctures from bottle to bottle, stirred, shook repeatedly, tested. Finally showed me the color in a little bowl, a wild green.

"Okay," I said again, "but what about the sorcery?"

"Yes," he said and reached for the brush. "What do you think they found on the girl, under her dead tongue?"

"I don't know."

"A ring."

In a single bold stroke Airborne drew a line on the back of my head. It made me think of a documentary film, with Picasso aiming in the same way and drawing steady lines.

"So, the archbishop feels relieved and puts the ring on his own finger." Airborne drew another line. "Now the emperor starts making eyes at the old archbishop, he yearns, he tries to force his way into the archbishop's bedchamber, he stands outside the door at night, he waits." Airborne laughs, with a gentle touch to my chin raises my head so I can see him and myself in the mirror.

"You have to picture it, these two old men, one in his vestments, the other in his emperor's robe, and the emperor wants to get into the archbishop's trousers." Airborne made the third stroke, then carefully repeated it. "Now, the archbishop's thinking what to do, wondering how can he stop this embarrassing situation. So, he throws the ring into Lake Constance. What happens? The emperor falls in love with the lake, he stands on the shore and he gazes, day and night he gazes out across the lake."

Airborne put the brush down, placed the little bowl with the wild green on the black granite slab. "You know what my friend says? True love, deep love that is, has to be one-sided, that's when the turmoil, the tension begins. If people love each other equally strongly, he says, then it's all as dull as dishwater. Don't you agree?"

"Actually, no. It depends what else you do beside loving. If you do nothing but love and work in insurance, then perhaps it gets a little dull. But if both are cave explorers. Or for instance, take that crazy Christo and his wife, they're a powerhouse the way both of them have been trying to wrap the Reichstag for twenty years. I think they could love each other equally strongly, but I don't think it would be like dishwater."

"Okay," he says, "you're right."

"What would you have done in the emperor's situation," I ask.

Without hesitating a second he says, "Put the ring on my own finger."

"For someone of your age that's not a bad idea. But for an old man it would be a depressing solution."

He took away my wrap, wiped the hair from the back of my neck with a wet cloth that smelled of sandalwood, got a mirror and showed me the back of my head. Three green streaks, below them the light stripes of my scalp, slightly slanting so that if you lengthened them they'd meet at my left shoulder, there where Airborne had massaged that knot, that tension. I tried to read in Airborne's face what he thought of this haircut. He looked satisfied with his work, even held his head slightly to one side.

"Say hello to Dr. Rosenow for me please."

At the cashier's desk where the other women working in this salon sat, I pay. One hundred and twenty marks. The most expensive haircut I've ever had. The boss with the maliciously grinning Butt-Head on his chest shakes my hand, says: "And think about it: never again a fade cut, least of all from an Ossie."

"Okay," I reply, "I'll keep it in mind."

I go out into the painfully harsh light, the oppressive heat. I turn around. The young men, the two young women are standing there looking at me. They're not laughing, as I'd suspected they would be, but are looking at me sadly serious, as if I'd just been driven out of Paradise.

Quickstep

OLD FRITZ THE EMPEROR IS RIDING DOWN
Unter den Linden, ahead of him the generals, behind,
right under the horse's ass, in bronze: Kant and Lessing. The horse turds would drop right on Lessing's
head. I walk, or rather, hop across the street. How
much I would have liked to sit down on one of those
linden boughs that, with their tender green, graze the
tops of double-decker buses. I can hear music, not the
Hohenfriedberg March, no, it's a foxtrot. The Caribbean
Dream seems to only just be taking effect, a kind of
slackness untypical of alcohol is taking over my arms
and legs. Foxtrot and Caribbean don't go together, I
think to myself and try a quickstep, slow, slow, quick,
quick, slow, over the cobblestones. I float along, in all
that crowd, that wild confusion streaming towards the
Reichstag. A woman's saying something to me, from
the side, getting in the way of my foxtrot. I say: "I give
for Tibet and Greenpeace and that's it, not a penny
anywhere else, got that?"

But the woman stays stubbornly, stays close. While I dance my way past the pedestrians, she goes on talking to me, a voice like seagulls shrieking. It only slowly penetrates, she doesn't want money, she wants to know something. "What?"

"Can I build a nest?"

"Don't want to," I say.

"Can you do that, build a simple nest, a nest like the bittern builds?"

"I'm not a bittern," I shout still lively and joyful and take some more steps, a waltz this time, that's right, a quickstep doesn't go at all with a foxtrot. Or does it? No bittern steps. This is more village swallows and the beautiful blue Danube, as beautiful as the blue Caribbean Dream. "Good heavens, that was a crazy mixture," I say.

"What," the woman asks, baffled.

"That blue Caribbean Dream. And then the Blue Peter, dios mios, did she have legs, sheer and going on forever. And don't you start talking to me about sexism, you can pour that over your handbag, for all I care."

"Listen," says the woman: "The bittern's nest in the reeds, what in comparison is such glitter, such vanity. All that sparkles, all that shines is only for Him, who shall be nameless, and for the Beast of the Seven Heads. You're still laughing," she says, "you're still hopping, but what will happen," she says, "when the End draws nigh? What then?" The woman now runs off to my right. She screams: "What then? What if the earth cracks open? What then?" The woman is turning beside me to my right. She screams: "What then?" The people ahead of us turn around before we reach them, her scream is that loud. "You are marked," she screams.

"Yes," I say, "and I paid dearly for it, every stroke thirty marks, cutting and washing not included."

"Dross," she screams, "all is dross. The bittern's nest in the reeds." More and more people stop, stare at us, I try to get away fast, but she stays by me. I turn into Charlottenstraße, step on it even more, she starts pulling at the sleeve of my jacket which I'm carrying over my arm, something crackles, sparks fly, a shock makes me start, so much had this woman charged herself up in her ash-can grey coat, a coat out of some synthetic material probably made in Novosibirsk, like her synthetic shoes with their glaring orange plastic soles. Probably one of those emigrants who for over two centuries held on to German and to some sectarian Bible interpretation in the Siberian tundra. Yes, she's sending out sparks, her hair stands on end, and she's talking about the lamb and trumpets; she sends out sparks every time she comes into contact with a passerby not wearing rubber soles. "Sin," she says, "Armageddon," she says, "Jehovah," she says, "the bittern's nest."

"For God's sake," I say as she stretches out her hand to me again and tugs my silk jacket, sparks flying. "Cut it out! Let go! Take your hands off me!"

At last, the Hilton. Putting on the jacket, the one I
paid so dearly for, I storm past the porter who spins the
revolving door for me, but bars the way to the pursuing
Avenging Angel in the Novosibirsk coat. Inside I come
to a halt, at last somewhere where it's pleasantly cool,
and see her standing outside, hands pressed against the
brown-tinted glass pane, trying to catch a glimpse of
me inside. I look in one of the mirrored columns to try
and see from my reflection what might have moved the
obsessed woman to persecute me of all people. Seen
from the front there's nothing that would draw attention, I decide. My hair is cut unusually short, I see
clearly what I'd already noticed with Rosenow, those
light patches on my face where the skin covered by my
hair wasn't tanned. Perfectly normal. If I turn my face
to the left though, I can see the ends of the three wild
green streaks. I'm marked, no doubt about it, but only
in a fashionable sense, I think. Or is there a place in the
Bible where three green streaks play a role? Normally
all these speople do is stand around with their *Watch-
tower* and smile promisingly at you. Perhaps it really is
because of the Caribbean Dream, because of my dance
steps, perhaps with the back of my head streaked green
I really do radiate the spirit of the Whitsun carnival.

I walk through the lounge, looking out for a man
with a pilot's case bearing the label: Hermes. There's
no man with a pilot's case in sight. The people sitting
here are in groups at the tables. Anyway, I'm here at

least half an hour early. At one table I see a writer I know, he's sitting there with a television editor I also know, both smoking cigars. They don't recognize me. In any case they've only seen me—if at all—in profile. They're laughing, I don't know if at my haircut or just because of something they're saying. With the two of them before my eyes, especially that literary prose-writing bumpkin with his cigar, I resolve to give up smoking not just when I've finished writing the article, but after I've smoked the four cigars still in my cigar case.

I sit down in the smoking area at a round table as far as possible away from the two. But I've no sooner sat down than I feel so sleepy, it takes a real effort to keep my eyes open, first Rogler's Dream then that iridescent blue Caribbean Dream, in which no doubt certain other substances were mixed. I must have dozed off for a moment because a waiter said quite firmly: "If you want to sleep, sir, would you please go to your room." People at neighboring tables are staring at me. Some are grinning. Probably I had been gently snoring, something I mostly do, I'm told, when I sleep sitting up.

I order a cappuccino and light a cigar. Carefully first heating the side with the match. Fernando Ortiz writes: Nicotine stimulates the mind by diabolically inspiring it. He's right!

The man comes through the lounge, small, fat, bald with dark bushy eyebrows sitting like bird's wings on his forehead. Accompanying him is a tall athletically-built man. Both are wearing beige summer suits. The stocky man is carrying a pilot's case. Even before I can wave they come over to me. I get up, say the password, Potato, and hold out a hand to the stocky man. It's not him but the athlete who takes it with his left hand, holds mine tight while his right shoots under my jacket, frisks my hips, my backside, quick and businesslike strokes, my member, this all happens so quickly I only just manage a stammered: "Now look, really, please, just a minute," before he, with an "Excuse me," pulls my tortoiseshell cigar case from my jacket pocket and opens it. He takes out a cigar, breaks it open, again says "Excuse me please." Pushes the case back in my pocket, bows slightly and moves to two tables away where, without letting me out of his sight, he sits down.

"Now look here," I say to the stocky man with the brushes on his forehead, "what is this, this is plain assault." But my outrage literally collapses when the man lifts his case onto the table and beckons me.

"The little box," I ask.

He nods. "Makinsurewedontgottacomplications," he looks at me questioningly.

"What?"

"Isprecaution—Excusinplease."

He puts his hands on the case. He has strikingly broad fingernails, real shovels, they're cut to a pointed oval, probably to make them look longer. The fine skin on the bed of three of his nails has been bloodily cut into. And I think, good Kramer didn't also give me a manicure.

"Did you get the catalogue from a taxi driver?"

He nodded. "Butyoutellinmefirstwhatyouthinkin."

"And you've the little box in your pocket?"

He nodded again.

"Wonderful," I said. "Do you realize it's valuable, you see, because of the classification of the different potato varieties, their characteristics: nutritional value, taste, susceptibility to potato disease."

"Yesyes." He shook his head. He laughed again, loudly, appealingly candid: "Isquestionofprice."

"There's the reward for finding it. It's really more a case of what it's worth ideally to me."

He shook his head. "Idealisgood—donowwham-bamthenover."

"Can you show me the catalogue?"

He shakes his head, says, "Isbussinessontrust."

"Do you have it with you?"

He shook his head again, but tapped the suitcase to confirm.

"Are you from Hungary?"

He nodded, but then said, "Bulgaria."

"Not Hungary?"

He nods. "No. Bulgaria."

I decided something in the Caribbean Dream was having a delayed effect, something that muddled all the

At the Reichstag thousands upon thousands of curious people are gathered, the sun shines in the grey-silver material; lashed down with ropes, the folds throw soft shadows, a huge wrapped-up parcel, that's what the Reichstag is now, a monstrous crate, ugly, bulky, flashy, I never could stand this crate, I always said you could already see the 1914 "Citizen's Truce" written all over the outside, now wrapped, this monstrosity is a wildly beautiful sight. Women, men, families with children and dogs, newspaper vendors, street traders, pieces of the Wall are still being sold, fingernail-size, palm-size, painted, blue, red, and military caps from the Red Army, from lieutenant to marshal, after all the Russians lost the war. Night goggles, tank clocks, medals, even the highest, the Order of Lenin, the Karl Marx Order are being gotten rid of here. Next to them living tableaux, mummies, Caesars, gilded putti, angels. I push my way through the crowd, how many films have a scene like this one that I've stumbled into. Rogler's Dream. I turn round again. The beige athlete is nowhere in sight.

Wannsee

THE WIND BLEW THROUGH THE OLD WOMAN'S yellow-brown hair. All the windows were pulled down in the old S-Bahn carriage from the thirties whose wooden benches had been upholstered in light green foam rubber and pine-green plastic covers back in the GDR era. Apart from the old woman and myself there were two boys in the carriage. They were standing at the door they'd opened during the journey, which of course was forbidden, just as I'd done as a child with Dickenmeyer on the way to Blankenese where we searched for the source of the Orinoco on the Banks of the Elbe. Both boys had put their beach bags on an empty bench. They were probably coming from afternoon school and were now going to swim. The old woman, who sat opposite me, was staring intently out of the window. The train stopped. Next to the station were allotment gardens with wooden sheds. Two small children were splashing in an inflatable blue plastic pool. Under a cherry tree a table was set, cups, plates.

An older woman was carrying a baking tray, probably with crumb cake, to the table, a young woman was pouring coffee, and an old man in a deck chair was reading a paper. The train had barely come to a standstill when it grew stiflingly hot. Sweat ran down inside my shirt collar.

"They want to tear all that down, them sheds. Get rid of them," said the old woman, as she kept looking out of the window. "They say it was illegal building here after the war."

At last the train started again, the wind streamed through the window, warm, but it still cooled. The two boys pulled the door open again so the wind started blowing once more in the old woman's hair, hair that was badly dyed, a ragged yellow-brown. I guessed she was in her mid-sixties, but perhaps she was older. She wore a fifties blouse with stitched pleats, the white nylon had yellowed. The old woman turned to the boys at the door, gave them an angry look. The boys paid no attention, they chatted and laughed. The woman was holding a shopping bag on her lap, imitation leather. There was a thermos flask in the side pocket.

"Are you going for a swim," I asked to distract her from the boys.

She looked at me in astonishment, for an instant her face relaxed, then became rigid again with her "No."

"I'd like to swim a bit," I said. "Could you tell me the best place?"

"Where do you whanna get out," she asked suspiciously.

"I think there's a bathing place at Wannsee."

"Then you godda get out at Nikolasee, when you leave the station, go right over the bridge, then straight to the lake, then you'll come to the Wannsee beach."

"I've been looking forward to getting into the water all day," I said. "In this heat. You're not going there?"

She looked out of the window a moment, then she said, "No, I can't swim."

"Didn't you learn to swim?"

"Nah, not really, and then that thing happened."

"What?"

"A group leader of the League of German Girls, she pushed me in. Gave me an awfool shock and I swallowed lotsa water, I went under. I," she hesitated, "I didn't like to go in the water after that. Later they gave the group leader a lifesaver's medal because she pulled me out." The old woman laughed uneasily, shook her head.

I told her I was once talked into jumping from the five-meter diving board. I stood up there and looked down. Everybody was shouting: Come on, jump! But I didn't. I climbed down again and they all laughed, all of them, everybody, the boys, and the swimming instructor. After that I was considered a coward.

"Did you never jump after that?"

"I did, later. A friend told me how to do it, don't

look down but in front at the water and say to yourself, I'm going to fly, that's a wonderful feeling."

"Yes," she said and looked out of the window, "that must be nice."

"Are you going to a barbecue?" I pointed to her bag.

"No," and for the first time she laughed, "no, I've never been to a barbecue." Again the harsh lines on her forehead showed. "It's terrible the way those Turks sit around the Reichstag making fires. It smells of burned fat and then the mess."

"The Turks pack everything away carefully. I think it's more likely to be our German young people who leave beer cans lying around everywhere."

"That's what you say," she again looked hard out of the window, as if she were now letting me know she considered the conversation closed.

One of the boys at the door held up a spray can behind her back. They both laughed, pointed to the woman's untidy yellow-brown hair as if they wanted to spray it blue. I grinned, slightly turned my head so they could see the green streaks. Both stuck thumbs up in the air in recognition.

The woman tapped the windowpane with her finger. "In the war they reloaded freight trains here. Very rare plants grow around here, I read it in the paper, from everywhere in Europe, wherever the German army was: France, Italy, and Russia." She unscrewed the thermos flask. "Would you like some, it's lemon tea, it quenches the thirst. I have to drink a lot in the heat, I've a heart condition."

For a moment I hesitated.

"I've another clean cup," she said and took a plastic cup from the bag.

"Yes, thank you," I said, only now realizing how thirsty I was. She poured me some tea and it tasted exactly the way my mother made it when I was a child and went to the Elbe with Dickenmeyer. "It tastes sour yet sweet," I said, "and it quenches your thirst."

"Yes, needs proper sugar, lotsa sugar, that's the secret," said the old woman.

"This does one good," I said, "I've already been offered two cocktails today. The last time was at the barber's. The day before yesterday I was at a barber's, he cut three ridges in my hair. I had to have my hair cut a second time today."

"That's disgraceful," she said. I turned the back of my head to her.

"Good lord," she said, "it looks," and she began to laugh, quietly but then louder and louder, "looks like you leaned against a green fence." She wiped tears of laughter from her eyes. "Never saw anything like that!"

"Yes, and I was in a hair salon, and they had Caribbean Dream there, blue, it tasted good, but now I'm incredibly thirsty. And I can hardly say what I paid."

"Would you like another cup?"

"Thank you. If you're not having the tea yourself, I mean, you need to drink a lot."

"I can take some out of the refrigerator at the atelier."

"The atelier?"

"Yes, I clean there. It's a designer's studio." Coming from her, the word designer sounded strange.

"What do they make there?"

"Oh, lotsa stuff, frames for sunglasses, irons, heaters."

"Don't you have a pension?"

"I do, yes," she said, and she waved her head, "six hundred marks, that's for the birds." She looked out of the window. "Just come from my aunt. Is in an old-age home. Ninety. Can't walk no more and always has this burning in her mouth. She says the food in the home is too spicy. There's only two kinds of food, she says, and both are too spicy. Yes, when she eats it hurts her mouth, raging pain. And she has that ever since she had to sell her furniture, 'cause she got in a small room, with furniture from the home. That very day her mouth started burning. Can't bear the dentures anymore in her mouth. When I visit her she sits there cutting away at them dentures with a potato peeler."

The old woman laughed, shook her head. The next station was announced.

"Well," she said, "gotta go. You hava nice day now."

"Thank you."

She got up and went to the door where the two boys were standing. The train slowed down. The boys pulled the door wide open. I saw the woman's hair fluttering in the wind. One of the boys took out a blue spray can and held it up. He made a head movement that asked: "Shall I?" Then everything happened quick as lightning, the old woman grabbed the boy's hand, twisted his arm behind his back so that he had to bend forward. "Ow, damn it!" he shouted. The spray can dropped from his hand and rolled along the carriage that was just coming to a halt.

"Just learned that," said the old woman, "so watch out! Because next time!" She got out.

She turned again briefly and gave me a nod.

"Crazy," said the boy rubbing his wrist. "You don't expect that from an old granny."

He got the spray can from under a bench. There was a blue streak on his red T-shirt.

"She sprayed you," I said and couldn't help laughing.

"I think I did it when she twisted my arm, what a dragon, man."

The two boys came over to me and without any embarrassment peered at the back of my head, the boy with the red T-shirt that now had a blue streak and the other, smaller boy, a bold ring in his ear and outsized trousers with sewn-on pockets.

"Cool," said the one with the gold ring in his ear, "megga cool."

"That green. Where'd yah gedit?"

"It was a pretty expensive joke," I said evasively.

"What did it cost."

"Sixty marks," I lied.

"That's cheap, man."

"Are you going swimming?"

"Later. We wanna spray first."

"Spray what?" The boy with the gold ring took the towel out of the bag with his swimming things and let me look in it. There were gloves and spray cans, red, black, and yellow. Amazing, how ready they were to show me all this and tell me about it. It was the three green streaks that had bonded us so quickly.

The boy with the red T-shirt pulled two stencils from the bag. "We cut them ourselves."

One of the stencils showed a cow. Under it the inscription: "I have seen Berlin. Take me home to my shed."

The other stencil portrayed a Neanderthal head with a speech balloon: "I like Adolf!"

"And where will you spray?"

"That's obvious, man, where it's forbidden."

"And the gloves?"

"Very important. If they catch you there's no fingerprints on the can."

"They've said it's okay on a fence on a building site,

they even try and get you to spray there. Man, that's for kindergarten kids on a day out."

"We've got a target, it's the polished granite in Friedrichstraße. They guard it day and night. But we'll get through."

"So what are you doing here?"

"Nothing. I wanted to work. To write something."

"What?"

"About potatoes."

That made them laugh, they couldn't believe it.

It made me laugh too. "Yes. I think I'll give up. Right now I'm on the run."

"What's that? Who's after you?"

"An arms dealer."

"Are you kidding?"

"Me. No."

"Man, that's cool. What are you going to do now?"

"Swim, that's the first thing."

Nikolasee Station. They showed me the direction: round to the right, then over the bridge. They had their eyes on a gleaming white garden wall. That's where they were heading with cow and Neanderthal man.

By the lake there really was a strip of light sand, though only narrow. It smelled of resin, burned grass, and—how to describe it—of blue, a blue slowly catching the warm brown evening breeze, if colors have a smell, that is. On my way to the beach under the pines and oaks I ran into day-trippers coming from there, on foot and cycling, laden with bags, blankets, and coolers. Gleaming red faces. There were only a few people left on the beach. The sun was low, its orange glow fell smoothly over the water, only splintering into fragments where some girls and boys, waist-deep in the water, played at knights on horseback. The girls were riding the boys' shoulders, legs tight round the boys' bodies. They were trying to push each other over. And they all let loose and shrieked when one of them fell into the water. I took off my shoes, socks, trousers, white shirt, only keeping on my shorts and waded into the water, slowly: it was cold, surely only an illusion because I was so hot, the water smelled of algae and duckweed. It made me think of Kubin's waterbed, of that despairing search for the greatest possible gratification that always leads to ever greater disappointment precisely because you're always denied what you're looking for, perfect happiness.

I swam, dove, the water green, bottomless. I swam far out, let myself be carried like a dead man on his back. The sun hung in the treetops like a fat orange, while up came the moon, wasted to a pale sickle.

Drawing a deep breath

I RETURNED TO THE HOTEL TO CHANGE MY shirt and trousers, they were sticking to my legs.

In my room I found a note that had been pushed under the door: Dial this number and give the operator the password: I need a boomerang call. Good luck!

I showered, put on jeans and a clean polo shirt. I ordered tea from the man who works as a porter in the hotel in the afternoon.

"Would you like Darjeeling or a weak Assam?"

"Assam, please."

"Take a seat in the lounge, I'll bring you the tea. By the way, there have been two phone calls for you."

"Who from?"

"They didn't leave a name. But they were foreigners. One of them, if I understood him correctly, will phone again. And the other asked for our address."

This made my blood run cold because I immediately thought of the Bulgarian and his beige gorilla.

"Please, if they phone again, under no circumstances give them my private address."

"I understand. Investment advisors," the porter asked.

"Yes. Something like that." I went into the lounge that served as the breakfast room in the morning. The French door to the balcony was open. You could hear voices and the noise of traffic from the street. On the sofa by the reading table sat a man in a crumpled black linen suit, leafing through the book Christo and Jeanne-Claude had published about the wrapping.

"Have you been to the Reichstag yet?"

"Yes."

"A crazy thing to do, simply crazy, I like it very much," said the man.

"Yes," I said, "so do I."

"Things are not going to be the same after this, I'm convinced this wrapping has seen to that. Things can be different, that's the secret. Incidentally, it hasn't occurred to any of these critics that the wrapping ends on the 23rd of July, Midsummer Night, that's when chaos reigns, confusion, disguise, role reversal are the order of the day. It's the most aesthetic night of the year. Things reveal another side, so do people. Miss Cobweb and Mistress Peaseblossom send greetings. If you want to meet them you'll have to come to a reggae concert tonight."

For a moment I wondered whether I should tell him

I'd already met Mistress Cobweb, but instead asked him the name of the bar.

"There's a band, they play a good mix of hip-hop and reggae, some boys from Jamaica, they'll stir up the primeval dreams in your cerebrum, but gently. Where are you from, if you don't mind me asking?"

"I'm from Munich. And you?"

"I'm from Hamburg, but I'm a Berliner."

"And I'm a Hamburger."

He laughed. "That fits."

"Did you come to see the Reichstag wrapped?"

"That's a coincidence," said the man, "if ever there was one, I've a world premiere tomorrow."

"Are you in theater?"

"No, I'm a composer."

"And what is this world premiere?"

"I've called it a requiem. It's called *Aspiration*. I've experimented with various instruments, instruments in the broadest sense of the word, for example, breathing aids for asthmatics, bellows for a blast furnace, also horns without valves, an oxygen tent in an intensive care unit, all instruments that work with air, also the breath itself, but not as speech, simply as breath."

"And who's this requiem for?"

"For Rosa Luxemburg."

"That's unusual," I said, "certainly right now. A few years ago when people read her work, carried her picture in the streets on banners, maybe, but now?"

"That's just the point," he said, "then it wasn't nec-
essary, she was alive, I mean people read her, discussed
her work, women's groups named themselves after her,
I don't mean that prescribed GDR veneration, the interest, the curiosity was voluntary. Then it wouldn't
even have occurred to me. But then two, three years
ago I saw a photo in the paper. A pig's head, split
open. Someone had placed it at the memorial where
Rosa Luxemburg's body was thrown into the Landwehr
canal. And then I thought, I have to return to this city I
left twenty years ago, I have to write this requiem which
is also for this city."

"Isn't that—please don't take offense—rather difficult?"

"Yes. It's an attempt. And it's extreme, I know. But
the attempt has to be extreme, otherwise all you have is
something bland and nice. Better an extreme failure," he
laughed. "I reread Rosa Luxemburg and I've really only
just now understood her, that attempt of hers to com-
bine, to reconcile what of itself is irreconcilable: equality
and freedom, to balance the two, in other words politics
ad infinitum, to bring about a reasonable balance between the needs, skills, interests, desires, constraints,
that outrageously stupid injustice contained in the word
natural—you know she had a severely dislocated hip—
to counterbalance this natural injustice against a social
right to equality, without however seeing human beings
as merely social material, on the contrary, safeguard-

ing the individual's integrity precisely because of his
uniqueness. I thought, this is what I must thematize
acoustically. I've read her articles, speeches, letters, particularly the ones she wrote from prison, love letters of
a—I can only use old-fashioned language—of a melancholy chastity. I've been to all the places here in Berlin
where she lived and worked. I recorded my breathing,
people think if you move at an even pace it's even, but if
you listen carefully it changes, not just because of the
slight alterations of pace but also because of what you're
hearing, seeing, feeling, and thinking. On the Schloß-
platz where she spoke, in Barnimstraße where she was
imprisoned and planted a lilac in the yard, the Hotel
Eden where she was ridiculed and beaten, the Lichten-
stein Bridge from which she was thrown into the canal,
the lock where her body was pulled out three and a half
months later, Friedrichsfelde Cemetery where she was
buried, the grave razed by the Nazis in '33, and where
later a politburocrat like Ulbricht set a plot aside for
himself. She was a strong little woman, it's tempting to
say delicate, but no, she was strong, powerful, solid but
injured, if you see the picture of her together with Clara
Zetkin, both wearing those hats, you can see if you look
closely: she's limping. I paced the same ground, also
with the memory of faded hopes, my breathing ringing
in my ears. I should tell you I once wrote a piece in '69 for
the shawm. It was to replace one of those simple
marches, something more or less new that people hadn't

heard before, but specifically for this instrument which was the instrument used by trackmen to warn of approaching danger. It was meant to be a kind of agitprop play in music. But it didn't interest the workers, for whom I'd written it, nor the labor unionists, nor the organized communists. They thought it was ghastly. To say nothing of the masses. It was a false start. It's not a question of trumpeting political messages, but of creating the aesthetic preconditions that make political action possible, moreover in a way that highlights the diversity and the uniqueness of the activity."

The porter came with the tea, placed it on the table, and said, "I've already put the tea in. I'd take it out in three minutes."

"Thank you," I said and asked the man in the black linen suit: "Who listens to your work now?"

"The ones that are interested, let's put it that way. Not many. Only a few. Are you familiar with contemporary music?"

"Hardly. Sometimes a friend, a book dealer and saxophonist with whom I play tennis, brings me CDs, the last time was from the Donauschingen festival. I'd like to hear your requiem."

"It's a minor work. If you like, come to the premiere tomorrow."

"Unfortunately I have to return to Munich tomorrow."

"If you're interested I can play you something. I have it on cassette. The equipment here isn't the best, but it'll give you an idea."

"I'd like that," I said, "then I can quietly drink my tea, if that doesn't disturb you."

"Not at all. It's a pity the arts are heard and seen in such isolation today. People should give readings, make music, drink coffee, and talk all at the same time. Do you listen to music when you're working?"

"Yes, sometimes."

"What?"

"Jazz, classical, hip-hop."

"Are you in advertising?"

"What gives you that idea?"

"Well, your haircut."

"I had it cut today. I wanted to do some research on the potato, I've experienced some pretty curious things in the process. You begin with the potato and end up somewhere quite different and on the way become someone different, as my head shows."

He laughed. "Good stories are like a labyrinth."

"Yes," I said, "but I lost the thread. All I still want to know is what Red Tree means. Do you know of a type of potato called that?"

"No. How'd you come by that name?"

"I came by it from an uncle of whom I was very fond. He could taste potatoes. I mean, he could tell the taste of the different varieties even when they were cooked. When he was dying he said: Red Tree. And nobody knew what he meant."

"At some stage I'll write a vocal piece made up of last words. You know them: More light, as Goethe said. Or perhaps Chekhov when he was lying in bed in Badeweiler, sat up and said in German: I'm dying. He fell back and died. But there aren't just short exclamations, a word or two, some people die talking. It's a project for voices."

"I'd really like to hear your work."

He went to his room. I poured myself tea, added some milk.

He came back with the cassette, put it in the recorder, balanced the speakers.

"Of course the speakers here aren't the best."

I was comfortable in the armchair, I lit a cigar, drank tea, and listened: the breath, even breathing, so it seemed, but then I heard a slight variation, a beat skipped, a breath held, only a second, then speeding up, a short cough as if something were being spat out, then regular again, lapped by a mighty, a frightening hissing, perhaps from bellows, bellows of a huge size as I'd once seen them at a blast furnace, a faint whizz like from a spray, a blowing, as the wind does, a mechanical gasping, a struggle for breath but also a deep drawing in of breath, a breathing out—the breath of the world.

The boomerang call

TOWARDS EVENING, AT A MOMENT WHEN THERE was no one in the lounge, I dialed the number the young man had written down for me. The number, I'd looked it up, was the code for Trinidad. Distant atmospheric crackling, or was it the tension in the transatlantic cables, then I heard a voice that said in strongly accented English, "Operator. Can I help you?"

I said what the young man had given as a password: "I need a boomerang call to Germany."

"Okay. The number please."

I gave Tina's business number. That was all. I thought at first I'd have to give a long explanation about how I had the number or the password. But nothing of the sort. The voice only asked whom to credit for the boomerang call. I gave the hotel's number.

"Fifty dollars per minute, it's okay?"

"That's fine," I said and thought, if that's true it's fabulous. The number was dialed, from distant Trinidad and Tobago where even as a child I'd wanted to go because I liked the stamps so much, the English King George in profile above palms, sandy beaches, and reed huts. I'd have to speak for about eight minutes, then the money would go back into the hotel's account. If what I'd been told, which sounded rather fanciful, was true. Was it the young man's friend or a place that could always be reached? I kept my eyes on the meter, and it did in fact quickly count 15, 16, 17 units, in a rhythm at yesterday's pace when I'd phoned Tina at her special number. Possibly even now it was still all being charged to the hotel. On the other hand, with a tariff of fifty dollars the amount would have increased so rapidly, the meter would have exploded. I figured just about anything was possible. I'd read there were forged credit cards in circulation with which you could make endless calls from any phone booth anywhere to anywhere in the world—all for free. Unthinkable four, five years ago when you still had to insert groschen and marks into the slot for the good old post office.

Tina answered, in that clear friendly voice said: "Hello." But I was really disappointed when I realized the voice was taped, so not her at all, at least not at that very moment. Also no shrieks, no groans, no sound effects. Perhaps the operator had listened fascinated before connecting me. He wouldn't have needed to know German for that. I heard her voice on the answering machine, businesslike, friendly: "I'm sorry I can't take your call right now. If you've any special requests, please leave a message. Take your time, you won't be cut off." So, I thought, she charges the special tariff on the answering machine too, there's no limit to her business acumen. I gazed at the little white box, and in fact after the meter had quickly counted thirty-one units, it and her voice suddenly stopped. I'm technologically illiterate, but it wouldn't have surprised me if the numbers had run backwards, I was actually even hoping they would, but they didn't. The number 31 stayed as if it had stuck. Then came the beep. I said: "Hello, this is Block. I'm sorry I couldn't come to the pool yesterday, but perhaps we could meet today. If you'd like to and have the time. I suggest a bar someone recommended to me where I'm told they play good reggae. Just a moment, I have to look for the address."

I looked at my wristwatch and would have dearly liked to know how this scam worked, a sound vacuum that earns money

....
....
....

The young woman whose orgasm I'd listened in on through the wall came down the corridor, hair washed, heavily made-up, a hand holding her dressing gown together over her breasts. She came into the lounge, saw me sitting there, receiver to my ear, listening, not saying anything, as if someone was in the midst of telling me something exciting. "Hello," I said and pressed the receiver to my chest, my heart, said: "I'm sorry, I've nearly finished my call."

"Yes," she paused in irritation, then said: "I only need to make a short call. To order a taxi. We're going to the theater."

"If you wouldn't mind waiting," I looked at my watch, "four minutes."

She gave a surprised and rather forced laugh, said, "All right, would you please just knock on our door." Then she went down the corridor back to her room. I lifted the receiver from my chest. She'll have heard my heartbeat, I thought. Perhaps she'll have heard me talk. Will she have understood it, that deep-chested roaring, my breath? I decided to test this when I was back in Munich, to phone a friend and ask him to press the receiver to his chest and speak. I held the receiver, listened, nothing. I brushed the receiver over my cropped head, then over the raised fabric of the wallpaper, acoustic fireworks for her, the acoustophile, something she'd perhaps enjoy. I let the pages of the phone book swoosh past the receiver, the wind through a train window, I rustled a napkin, leaves blowing in, rubbed the receiver over the cloth of my trouser leg, perhaps now she's getting goose pimples and again I saw the blond down. The hand on my watch showed there was still a minute to go:

. . . .
. . . .
. . . .

I gave the name of the bar, added: "I hope we'll see each other tonight." I was pretty sure she wouldn't come, possibly she'd simply hung up during the silence without waiting for the address. But perhaps she'd been curious enough to keep the receiver to her ear for eight minutes. I laughed softly but so she could still hear, not that I did it intentionally, it was the thought of her listening while the meter ran on, a pretty disgusting pleasure I was taking, Schadenfreude, gloating, that national characteristic of which people accuse the Germans. I didn't care, at least not just then, because I figured this was only getting even, she'll have had her fun at the thought of me in that heated pool for senior citizens. "Those who dig a ditch for others to fall in, do well," I said and hung up.

The tears in things

A BLACK MAN—HUGE, SHAVED HEAD—TOOK A hard look at the people coming in, let me through into the booming darkness, drumming, the drummers glistening with sweat, gasping as they drum, men and women dancing slowly as in a dream, others sitting or standing. A few tables, chairs of social realism ugliness, gigantic amplifiers, the most expensive, the newest, that blare out waves of sound. I pushed my way past the people standing around—many Blacks, a few Whites, mostly women—and leaned against one of the cast-iron pillars. A girl came, her thighs squeezed together by a tight red leather skirt, her hair a gaudy purple, she pressed a beer bottle into my hand, "beer from Jamaica, genuine," she yelled in my ear, "that's eight-fifty."

"Giving me an Oktoberfest price!"

"Yeah, but you don't pay no cover charge here and you can ogle all you want—old Peeping Tom that you are anyway." She laughed, made no move to give me change for my ten marks.

As I'd expected, Tina hadn't come. Two women were dancing, lightly swaying their hips they caught the drumbeat shock waves, absorbed them, turned them, let them slowly glide through their arms, their thighs, legs, led them through their fingers out into space, their bodies moved, only their heads stayed still while mine bobbed up and down.

A young woman came over to me, bare shoulders, a really short metallic silver dress hanging on its spaghetti straps, too-high wedgies, also silver, darkest pitch-black hair, the long bangs falling into her eyes made-up to their darkest black—and in that blackness, the iris blue. She smiled at me. The face seemed familiar, for a moment I thought it was the young woman from the hair salon.

"You won't let your head go," she shouted in my ear, "that's why it's wobbling, the rest of you is rigid. That woman over there, her head isn't moving, the eyes, see, she's in a trance, the movement all revolves around the navel."

As a matter of fact, I could see her navel under the man's shirt she'd tied in a knot.

"You're right," I yell back, "it's like a center of stillness."

One of the women had hair that was dyed fiery red and teased up high in some mysterious way as if it had exploded above her head. The other woman, dark-skinned, looked like a saleswoman at a make-up counter, boredom carefully painted on her face, but here in action, slowly she flailed her arms, her Wonderbra breasts swaying in slow motion before my eyes.

"Have you got the taste catalogue back yet?"

I'd happily have swallowed back the idiotic Oh that came out of my mouth.

She laughed and said, "You're staring as if you had a screw loose." She pulled at her black bangs: "I got your message. I liked what you recorded for me, by the way."

I said something unimaginative—I had not recognized her under the wig.

"I didn't recognize you either. Pretty gutsy—that haircut at your age. But I like it."

"It was an emergency solution."

"Necessity is the mother of invention, as we know." She ran her hand over my hair. "Feels cool. You're wearing it just as short as me now."

"By the way," I said, "I'm really sorry I couldn't come yesterday. An old friend phoned."

"A pity," she said, "I was there."

I wondered whether to tell her I'd only seen elderly people. But then I thought, since she's lying now, it shows she hadn't just wanted to make me look ridiculous. Otherwise would she have come here now?

"Do you have a cigarette?"

"No. You can have a cigar."

"They're too strong for me." She balanced her way on high platforms over to a table and spoke to a young man. He held out a pack, gave her a light, said something to her, looked over at me, grinned, and pointedly shook his thick brown hair over his face. "Hairy asshole face," I said pretty loudly.

The girl in the red skirt was back again. "That beer is hitting your aggression glands, man," she said and pressed another bottle of Jamaica beer into my hand.

"Do you have fizzy water," I asked her.

"Man," she said, "that's all we need. We're doing this for the local industry in Jamaica." And she again pocketed the money as a matter of course without handing over any change. "By the way, there's chili con carne today, if you're weak in the knees."

Her manner had changed, not a good sign, I put it down to my age and as a rejection. I shouldn't have asked for fizzy water.

Tina came tottering back in her metallic miniskirt, the lit cigarette between her fingers. "I read your ad for the catalogue in the paper. Did anyone show up?"

"Yes. A man."

"And?"

"He wanted to sell me mines."

"Mines?"

"Yes. Fragmentation mines. Land mines. Explosive mines. I could even have bought anti-tank mines. Today I learned that arms dealers call mines potatoes."

"Crazy," she said. "You know what occurred to me after you called," she said. "I had time to think when I played back your message. We could do this exhibition together. The material's here. Rogler would love it. We'll have a tag line: The Joy of Tasting. Or something like that. The potato through the centuries."

"Yes," I said, "why not, great," it slipped out of me sounding really enthused.

"No, I wouldn't enjoy it. Maybe yesterday. Yesterday was a wild day."

"And today?"

She looked at me, softly blew smoke in my face. "Yeah, today too!"

This gave me goose pimples, something that hasn't happened to me in years.

She looked at me out of those hellishly dark-ringed eyes, the irises not just blue, but set into them like stars are fine light green stripes. The lashes that shaded them were stuck on.

With a piercing shriek the band stopped. I felt I was plunging into a sudden emptiness, a stillness, but then a moment later all the other sounds swelled up like a flood, laughter, talk, the clink of glasses.

"So you didn't find out if it was a potato variety, Red Tree?"

"No."

"I'm really sorry about Rogler's work."

"Yes." How could I have described my feeling of shame to her, one so acute that I kept trying to push it aside, forcing myself to think of something else. And what was I going to tell Rosenow? I'd decided to write him a letter from Munich offering to find a similar Biedermeier box for him. That would be a replacement, but there could be no replacement for Rogler's taste catalogue. It was Rogler's life.

"Do you know where this is from: Things too have their tears," I asked her.

"No."

She leaned over with her ear near to me; as I saw from close up the black wig was real hair, the delicate flat ear smelled like a calyx, a heavy sweet perfume. I felt her hair in my face and now and then the touch of her ear into which I was speaking, lengthening the vowels because I knew then her two tiny muscles contracted: Things too have their tears. "A friend said that to me over thirty years ago. For years I tried to find out where the quotation came from. Last summer I was in New York, Greenwich Village, I was living on Bleecker Street. I was sitting in an apartment, writing, heard the police cars howling like dogs, ambulances with their electronic yodeling. I wrote and wrote as if I were being carried along by all this non-stop commotion, as if I were soaring. From time to time I had to get up to feel the ground again under my feet. I went to the window, a large window with a panoramic view, and looked out over the square where the New York University students were playing tennis, jogging, doing gymnastics. It was the day for special activities for the disabled,

Wednesday afternoon. Two deaf-mutes were practicing karate, a Chinese woman, small, muscular, not in a rigid sinewy way, but delicately rounded, and a middle-aged man, already grey, probably a professor. They were talking in sign language, especially the woman instructor whose job it was to explain the movements, how to hold the arms, how to stretch them, all in this energetic sign language, fingers spreading, fist striking palm, fists, arms circling. He'd then copy her a little awkwardly. Delicate birdlike signs became powerful calculated movements. It was a wordless poem, a poem of gestures. I reached to the shelf by the window where there were books the previous inhabitants had forgotten or deliberately left behind because they were simply too heavy for the journey back. I took down a book, *Distracted Looking* by Reinhard Lettau, opened it and at first glance found this: So he excused the military order in my kitchen with the Virgil quotation, that things too have their tears: a right to a regular place where they feel at home. Herbert Marcuse said this to Lettau, and since then I've known where this quote comes from that I heard some thirty years ago from a friend."

"Couldn't you just have asked the friend who said that?"

"That's just it."

"And why not?"

"He was shot here in Berlin twenty-eight years ago in June."

"God," she said, "that's almost two years before I came into this world." Quite unexpectedly she reaches for my head, strokes my hair, the way you do with children you want to comfort, gently reaches for the back of my neck, pulls my head to her, and kisses my temple. She holds the cigarette far from her so the smoke doesn't get in my eyes, though here the air is nothing but smoke, blue and heavy.

"And you think the little box is crying now?"

"No, I wasn't being that sentimental."

"I like sentimentality, it makes me feel so deep inside. And I like crying at the movies and at stories and wherever. It's typical of your generation to have no feeling for sentimentality. Frankly, it scares you shitless to live out your feelings. You as well. You talk about chaos, but everything just passes you by like water off a duck's back. Its only when you get really lucky that your world cracks. But usually somebody has to die first. Or leave you."

The girl in the red skirt comes back again and brings me a bowl. "Chili con carne."

"I didn't order it."

"What, don't you want it, I thought you needed it." Unfazed she holds the bowl out to me. "Twelve marks."

"I've got exactly the right amount."

"Good," she says, pulls a spoon wrapped in a paper napkin from her waistband.

I begin spooning up the chili. But it's hot and

fiendishly spicy. "Yes," I say, "I actually wanted to tell you a story about a friend on the phone. But only the answering machine was on."

"Do I know him," she wants to know.

"No, how should you? A friend in Munich. He's a statistician. Freelance, he works at home. From his window on the third floor he can see into the apartment opposite. In the summer a woman moved in there. Would you like some?" She nods. I hold out a full spoon to her, blow on it to cool it as you do for children. She takes the spoon in her mouth like a good girl, swallows. Nods. "Hot. Spicy." "Well. Now it's winter. The trees in the street have lost their leaves, so now he can see into the living room. A modernly-furnished living room, and through another window he can see into the corridor, from there into the bedroom. But he can only see a narrow section of the bedroom." I hold out another spoonful to her, she nods, takes the spoon into her mouth, right to the top, leaves some of her dark red, almost black lipstick on it. I take a spoonful, taste the cherry flavored lipstick under the burning chili, an extremely artificial fruit taste. "But sometimes, when the wardrobe mirror is open at a certain angle he can see the bed, a wide one. Now and then he looks up from his calculations and sees the woman going back and forth, until one evening he sees a man. He sees the woman and the man in the mirror, some quick movements, a shirt that drops down, a skirt, a shoe, the woman's

naked legs stretched out and the man's, the woman's
legs disappear from view. Nothing else. After this, he
stands every evening at his window and stares across.
And he discovers: different men go there, a real fancy
call girl, he thinks to himself. And depending on the
position of the mirror, sometimes all he sees are the
feet, sometimes the legs, but just once, almost, he sees,
but only almost, both bodies." I hold out the spoon to
her, she takes some, says, "My God, is this spicy." "The
man buys himself opera glasses, a week later expensive
binoculars, finally a pair with an infrared telescope for
night viewing. He locks himself in his room so that his
wife won't take him by surprise. He stands and waits all
evening for the woman's visitor, says to himself I'm a
Peeping Tom, thinks, the word voyeur is much too
weak for what I'm doing. If she doesn't have a visitor
he's disappointed, or rather, depressed and also bad
tempered with his wife and children. Would you like
another spoonful?" She shakes her head. "Now he can't
bear to be in the apartment, he runs around at night,
then rushes back home because he decides that at that
very moment she's having a visitor. But she's sitting in
front of the television. And one day he meets the
woman in the supermarket, an attractive, well-groomed
young woman and she looks at him and the way she
looks at him he suddenly realizes she knows he's been
watching her from across the way. And in fact that very
same evening the mirror's positioned in such a way that

he can see the bodies. What he sees, to his way of thinking, is wild abandon."

"Give me another spoonful."

"He waits for her, speaks to her. One time she takes
him to her place, just once he's there, opposite, up
there. He can see his apartment, his room, his window
from the outside. No tenderness, no talking, this is just
plain wild sex. After that she abruptly ends all contact.
The mirror stays shut. All he can see is the edge of the
bed. Now and then he sees men coming and going,
mostly elegantly dressed. They park their heavy
BMWs and Jaguars two blocks away, as he discovers.
Now he can hardly work. And when he does his concentration is so poor he makes mistakes, catastrophic
mistakes."

"Of course," she says, "I know the ending."

"Look," I say, "listen, this is my story."

She laughs. "Rubbish, it's one of those stories that
make the rounds, there are thousands like it. It's a really
trivial story."

"What? But I don't know how it ends."

The drums started up again, sudden explosive
shock waves aimed at the solar plexus.

"Oh," she yells in my ear, "one of my phone clients
always says there are no stories left. Only those that
people tell each other on the phone, he says as he winds
his watch."

"And how does it end then?"

"That's simple," she says. "One evening when his wife's watching television she hears a scream. Wonders what's going on. Looks around the apartment, calls her husband, goes into his room, the window's open. She looks out of the window. Her husband's lying below. Binoculars clenched in his hand. She looks up and sees a naked woman standing at the window opposite, waving at her. A really corny story, I couldn't offer that on the phone to anyone. What's the matter, you're crying."

"I think it's one of these green peppers. A rather pithy ending," I say and think to myself, no need now to write this story. Good, I decide. Yes, I'm relieved. I don't need a beginning anymore. What I have at home on the laptop I'll send into the void with DELETE.

"Has that story made you sad?"

"No. Not at all." I put the bowl down on a table. "I'm only sorry about the taste catalogue." My head is so battered by the Jamaica beer and the drumbeat shock waves I don't give a damn about anything. I slowly withdraw into myself, it feels good. The ceiling fan swirls smoke and hot air. The pressure of the reggae slowly makes its way down, forces the thoughts leaping around in my head out and down into my diaphragm.

On the dance floor, which is really only a small space not taken up by tables and chairs, the movements grow faster, the people move closer, bodies touch, men and women dance behind each other and in front of each other, now the woman with the fiery red hair is

dancing with a gigantic Black, a gold tooth with dia-
monds sparkles in his mouth, she turns, he dances behind her, by her circling buttocks which he almost but
not quite touches with his powerful thrusts.

"Come on," she says, "we're dancing." She dances
ecstatically, I have to concentrate hard, strange thoughts
are running through my head, such as: good thing you
jog every day, still, I hope you don't get out of breath too
soon, I hope you don't step on her, I hope she doesn't
sprain her ankle, those heels are unbelievably high. Suddenly she's dancing more slowly which I don't like at all,
I've only just got into my stride, now she's dancing with
those slow-motion movements that I'm just no good at, I
feel I'm like a jumping jack, she's dancing close to me,
comes closer, really close, her breath, that heavy flower
perfume blows on me, heavy, sweet, but when I want to
pull her closer she keeps her distance. And though the
dance floor is so packed with ecstatically dancing cou-
ples, there's no pushing, which is astonishing. But then
I get a powerful shove from behind and this time I fall
against her, or rather, onto her, feel her body delicate
and soft, for a moment it feels like I'm dancing with a
man, as if there was someting here that didn't belong
between a woman's legs. Her real-false hair flies, she
laughs, she waves her arms in the air like a conductor,
fast again.

It's an illusion, I tell myself, it has to be an illusion.

Perhaps it's just a sanitary napkin that slipped. Or one of those so-called intimacy bags for women when they travel or go to dangerous parts of the city, bags not worn round the hips anymore but between the legs, and apparently not just for security but because it feels good. I'd seen them in a shop on Houston Street, they looked like little sausages made out of suede. Only paper money fits in them, and you have to roll it. She was barely moving, holding back, but so relaxed, so effortless. The band stops. I gasp for breath, I'm sweating but feel something I haven't felt in years, I feel easy, her ease has infected me.

The waitress comes, again presses a bottle into my hand, says to her: "Hullo Tina, heresa beer," presses the other bottle into her hand. I pay. The waitress tucks away the twenty marks.

I hold back a comment, I don't want to seem petty. But I think to myself, the waitress knows her. So she often comes here.

"But you're wearing a ring today?"

"It was just given to me."

"You're quite a liar," she says.

"What makes you think that?" I say, outraged because I immediately remember how she stood me up yesterday and then today tells me she was at the pool.

She drinks from the bottle, looking thrillingly vulgar in that metallic silver dress. She links arms with me.

The hairy fop peers over at us, now with what I'd call a really randy look about his mouth. I give him a quick, contemptuously superior smile.

"You do a good crawl," she says, "and your catapult turn wasn't bad."

"What?"

"Yeah. But it was really funny when you swam into that old granny. She bobbed up and down in the pool like an old walrus."

She looks at me and begins to laugh, "Now you really do look, what'll I say, there are no words for it." She gives me a quick kiss. "Come to my place. When we're there I'll give you my work on the potato in literature."

I'm standing, the bottle of Jamaica beer in my hand. I take a swig from the bottle to sort out my thoughts, think, this Jamaica beer tastes horrible, think, a mixture of malt beer and wheat beer, think, so she was there, think, so she saw you, think, she was there, think, but where, think, she was watching you, think, I need to get out into the fresh air or I'm going to faint, think, I wasn't wearing my glasses but I can still recognize people on the other side of the street. So, think, I should have seen her, think, must have been somewhere, think, but where?

"You've wandered off with your thoughts again," she says, "I'm here." This is when I remember the rod and the boy, the blond boy dangling from the rod for a swimming lesson.

"Come on," she says, "we're going, I want to feel you properly, and when I say properly, that's what I mean." She looks at me, no friendly smile, grimly serious, out of the depths of her eyes made-up black and shaded by false lashes.

Fear of depths I think: I hear myself saying it aloud in my head: fear of depths.

"Yes," I say, "exactly."

"What," she asks.

"I have to go to the bathroom, this Jamaica beer."

"Okay," she says, "I'll wait here."

I push my way through the dancers, turn around one more time, she's looking in my direction, not mocking but serious, no smile, she's looking in my direction tense and serious. Or he is?

I go past the men's room door and through the swinging doors into the kitchen where a friendly Black in a white chef's hat is just emptying Chappy dog food tins into a pot with black beans.

I say: "Tasty, that chili con carne."

He nods, lifts the ladle as if he wants to let me have a taste. Laughs. I go past him, think, at least the story about the Chappy isn't just another of those corny stories, and go out through the kitchen exit.

Outside it's pitch dark.

The funeral orator

I STILL WANTED TO EAT A CURRIED SAUSAGE and I went to Bahnhof Zoo to a food stand that I knew stayed open at night. It smelled of rancid fat and the sausages under the electric grill had shriveled to the size of a little finger, the dark brown skin cracked and burst.

"Can you spare a mark," an elderly man asked me, who despite the heat was wearing an old crocheted cap that looked like a tea cozy. I gave the old man fifty pfennig. He thanked me with a vigorous shake of his head and wished me a successful night.

"Why successful?"

My question unleashed a raging tic in his face, "The heat," he said, "it's in my head, you can't get in, can't get in, the first wing is on its way, sawn off, it's broken, dust, the dust, there's dust in my skull, sleep comes out of the head," he got into a muddle: "the pyropython is wrestling, not the grey vulture." The rest of what he mumbled was incomprehensible.

I went to Runnerspoint, the food stand at the corner of Kurfürstendamm and Joachimstalerstraße, ordered a curried sausage. Next to me stood a man eating a rissole spread finger-thick with mustard.

When he saw my glance, he said, "Yes, it's my inspiration. If I run out of ideas I eat a rissole with a lot of mustard."

"What ideas do you need in the middle of the night?"

"I'm writing a speech. I have to give it in the morning."

"What kind of speech, if you don't mind my asking?"

"A funeral speech."

"Are you a pastor?"

"No, rather the opposite. I write speeches for people who don't want to be buried by a pastor."

I ordered a beer and took a bite of the curried sausage. I thought of my mother's death. She'd left the church; it wasn't an aggressive act, business was bad, she worried and she believed God wouldn't mind if she had fewer worries on his account by sparing herself the collection plate. Her death posed a banal question: how should I bury my mother? There had to be a structure, a form. After a life like hers you can't just go and sink a coffin into the earth. Should I say something at the funeral? But I was sure I wouldn't be able to do this because I know myself. I'd need all my concentration in order not to cry, and cry uncontrollably. Strangely

enough, for this to happen I always need other people
to be present, as well as the words, I have to express the
mourning, hear myself speak, and I begin to cry, otherwise it's only a paralyzing sadness, a pain mute and
heavy.

"I don't think it's easy," I said, "to always hit the
right note at a funeral."

He licked the mustard from his finger, then nodded.
"It depends," he said, "on what's expected. It depends
completely on the wishes of the bereaved, whether they
want to have it dry or wet." The funeral orator shoveled
more mustard onto his rissole. "The bereaved decide.
You soon get a feeling for it, whether they want to cry
or look forward to the inheritance behind a mask of serious concentration. Of course, you have to take a look
at the life of the deceased. But they don't give a damn
anyway what anyone does. There are cases though
where people set down in their wills what they want
said about their life. High points, belated justifications,
even spiteful digs, from out of the coffin, as it were.
Anything's possible." He ordered another can of beer,
tore off the seal, and drank. "Stimulating the tear ducts,
nothing's easier. Shakespeare knew that. And suffered
for it later. All you need is to let the bereaved tell you
the details, what was the deceased attached to, a canary
for example or"—he looked around—"an old crocheted
home-made tea cozy, possibly the only object an East
Prussian expelled from her Königsberger home was

able to save, a tea cozy that accompanied her, a girl of fifteen, on her flight over the frozen lagoon, that protected her as a hat against the piercing cold of January '45 on the whole long journey through Pomerania, right on to Berlin, where, when the Russians marched in, she pulled it down over her head with a warning that she had typhus, then the first real coffee given to her by a GI because of this hat that amazes him. Let's say he was from New Orleans. You don't need tea cozies there. The woman marries, has children, the children have children, so time goes by, but in summer on Sundays there's coffee on the balcony and the tea cozy's stuck over it, meanwhile it's been carefully mended a few times, it keeps the pot warm, a symbol of security, security and warmth, and that was what the deceased also gave to all—then you lift up the old tattered tea cozy and all the mourners swim out of the chapel on a flood of tears after the last blessing. A colleague of mine has this technique mastered to perfection. Sometimes she starts to bawl herself. Later of course the mourners wonder what got into them, they look at each other moved and embarrassed and have to wash down their embarrassment with a few glasses of schnapps. They can have the same thing from me. Of course. Whatever you want. A real workout. But a funeral, burial, or cremation can also be a relaxed affair where you sit back thinking your thoughts, you could even smoke a cigar. The old political left-wingers go for that." He licked the mustard from his index finger. He shook his head and said: "No, I'm not giving anything."

I turned round and saw that the beggar had followed me. He immediately began talking to me. I ordered him a curried sausage. "You know," he said and his left eye twitched: "that it was there, the anti-aircraft bunker, the zoo, the Russians come, hippos in the zoo dead. Monkeys burned, water ran out. Fish? On the ground like this," he twitched "and like this," and he twitched again. "Giraffes? Dead. Elephants? Dead. Dead! Dead! Dead! And the bunker? Boom, nonstop. Ack-ack up there, down here already the Russians. Boom. They shot from the roof. Boom. I came down, crocodiles dead. Boom. And the elephants dead. Dead."

"Right, now clear off," said the man behind the electric sausage grill; he handed the old man the paper plate with the curried sausage and waved him away. The old man walked away a few steps, stopped and started talking excitedly to himself again, paper plate with the curried sausage in his hand, but not eating it.

"Did you study comparative literature," I asked the funeral orator.

"No. What gives you that idea?"

"Because of the cigar, I was thinking of Brecht."

"No. I studied philosophy for a couple of semesters. Philosophy and Sanskrit. I quit in '68. Philosophy. That's a post-pubertal desire. Then I earned a living as a pallbearer. That's when I got to know this funeral orator, one of the old school who still wrote orations in verse. There were still people in those days who wanted to put close relatives in the earth with rhyme and reason. I stood in for him one day when he was supposed to say something about an atheist. This experienced funeral orator simply didn't have a clue. Because the man had killed himself, he'd hanged himself. But he was a communist. How did all that fit together? What to do? The bereaved, all staunch communists, wanted a political speech. What do you say? After all, they believe in the future. The man wasn't up to it in their eyes. So I stepped in. Quoted Bloch. Hope as a matter of principle. And said, suicide, it's our license to freedom. A moment of hope, yes, of smiling freedom lies therein. I had plenty to do in those days. People were leaving the church, after '68 a wave of them, that's when I went into business. A real boom. And comparatively easy. Life and society. Society was shitty, the capitalist reality, inhuman, life could be so much better. Brother to the sun, to freedom, and so on. And for the finale some powerful trumpet blasts: our license to be free. He fought, now he rests, but the fight goes on." He looked at me as he drank from the can. "What do you do? Entertainment business?"

"What gives you that idea?"

"Anyone with a haircut like that isn't working in a bank."

"True."

A van from the Workers' Samaritans Association pulled up opposite. A man was lying in the gutter, two men standing by him, you couldn't tell whether he'd been beaten up or hit by a car. The funeral orator looked over at him: "Another alcoholic in a coma," he said. "Yes, business has gotten pretty damn hard. All you can do is take a quick look at the biography of the deceased, society nada, future also nada. The competition from the church has it easier. The Bible's a handbook for social events. Whatever you're looking for, you'll find. And it's just this book we're forbidden to use in our work." He put the last piece of rissole in his mouth, wiped the mustard from his thumb and index finger with a paper napkin.

"Lately I can hardly cover my expenses."

A Tamil came to the stand, in one hand a bunch of red roses all already hanging their heads. He offered us a rose. He spread the fingers of his left hand. Five marks each. "No thank you," said the funeral orator. The Tamil looked tired and disappointed, probably he'd spent the entire evening going to restaurants and bars trying to sell his wilted roses. But maybe the roses had wilted on their journey through Berlin's nightlife because their preserving agent only lasted until just before midnight. I thought of Spranger, who perhaps had cut the stems of these roses slantwise with pruning shears. And, acting on an impulse, I bought a rose from the Tamil. In all the years up to now I'd always sent the rose sellers away with a shake of the head. Now for five marks I had a half-wilted, long-stemmed rose in my hand and didn't know what to do with it. I find it hard to throw flowers away, even when they're already wilted. I put the rose on the stand counter and planned to forget it there.

The Tamil pointed to a sausage, "No pork?" And shook his head in revulsion like a child. The food-stand man said: "Is no pork. Is real cow." He winked at us and said: "I've got in it for Allah. Allah is mighty, Allah is great, he's five feet tall and lazes around the Branden-burg Gate." He pushed the paper plate with the curried sausage over to the Tamil. "Whad I say is, you eat wot's putin front of ya. Yeah," he laughed at the Tamil. The Tamil laughed back, friendly, nodded, put the miser-able roses on the stand counter and began eating the curried sausage.

"Three years ago," I said, "when my mother died I wondered what, how should I put it, what form to give my mother's funeral. She'd left the church."

"And how did you solve it, I mean your mother's funeral?"

"I couldn't think of anything other than to ask the pastor of the Christus-Kirche where I'd been chris-tened. Which I found really embarrassing. Because I'd also left the church. He was a really nice pastor, open-minded, modern, for a time he'd been the pastor to some motorbike rockers. He gave an oration without any flourishes that was moving in a tactful way."

"Yes," said the funeral orator, "there's strong competition. Even critical people like you resort to the state churches, others simply have their relatives disposed of. Burned and then the ashes packed into small tins that soon corrode. The tins are buried unnamed. And now there's even competition from these trendy people. Now they're moving into the business, pop funerals, real stage productions, coffins lined in Christo's wrapping from the Reichstag. And video clips from the deceased's collection and techno junk to go with it, coffins with chromium-plated Harley Davidson jewelry, and an orchestra from the state opera playing 'Born to be Wild' by Steppenwolf. An exhilarating farewell celebration God calls it."

"God?"

"No, not God himself. The man's called God, Golo God, he manufactures coffins for the happy-death cult, it's not a pseudonym, God's his name. A person couldn't think up something like that, it really is his name.

The Tamil had eaten his curried sausage and offered us another rose. Perhaps he thought we were in a different mood or that by now I'd forgotten I'd already bought a rose. But perhaps it was a simple reflex and he just kept on offering roses. The funeral orator patiently shook his head.

"And in the East? Hasn't a new market opened up for you there? Many people in the GDR left the church."

"Good heavens, that was for tactical reasons. With us it's because of the dues, with them it was because of the party. Now they're letting themselves be buried again by the patient Protestant pastors. Or by old functionaries. You wouldn't believe the number of people from the former cadres who are now working as funeral orators. It's a solution, once upon a time responsible for agitation and propaganda, now they're giving their curriculum vitae a new angle. No, we won't get into the market in the East. The Ossies will still be looking for the good old days when the final trumpet sounds. Nothing to be done. I just have to supplement my earnings by doing something else on the side."

"And what are you doing now?"

"I switched to the piano. I play the piano at Sunday brunch in a trendy café. I learned to play as a child. My mother was always after me. Every day two hours' practice. I could never see what use it would be, but then there does come a time it does come in handy. I used to play in a student jazz band in the early sixties." He carefully wiped the last tiny bit of mustard from the paper plate with his middle finger. "I'd like to have buried that radical Marxist Dutschke, a pity, a Protestant vicar spoke on that occasion. Dutschke and Bloch. Do you live in Berlin?"

"No," I said, "I'm only here," I hesitated a moment, "I'm here on a visit."

"Where do you live?"

"In Munich."

"I'll give you my card. I also come to Munich, travel expenses paid, second-class."

"What does one of these speeches cost?"

"A thousand marks. Of course then it's a quite special, individual speech. You have to take into account that I need to talk to people first to get to know about the deceased person's life, also about the bereaved, no speech without substance. It's a matter of evaluating. A life's evaluation. Dying after all has plenty to do with the way a person lived. Death is the requiem. For instance, the speech I have to make tomorrow, I've been struggling with it for four days."

"Who's the deceased?"

"A retired teacher. He set it out in his will, no church representative, but a funeral orator. The institute doing the burial, for whom I often work, engaged me. The dead man's wife died years ago. The son, whom I phoned in Brussels, just said he'd already fallen out with his father when he was a student. The father had refused to finance his studies. I'm not coming, the son said, and my father wouldn't have come to my funeral either. Fathers are coincidental, then monsieur son wanted to give me a lecture on fatherhood over the phone and at my expense. Quoted Foucault. I thought, the horse is riding me. I interrupted him: what was your father like? And the son said, I'd prefer not to tell you because then you'd have to say bad things about him at the funeral. Thank you, I said and hung up. Then I asked neighbors in his building. The answers: unfriendly. Hardly said hello. Just looked at you bad-temperedly. So, and now make a speech out of all that. And then at the funeral, if they turn out, there's three people. I have to drink at least one hip-flask first, or I can't even bring myself to enter these places of last benediction. And schnapps costs. A pastor is paid for putting people in the earth, and he even receives a pension. But me, as a free-lancer. Well, if you ever find yourself in the situation, a phone call will do."

He dug a calling card out of his crumpled black linen jacket. "If you're interested, come to the funeral tomorrow, eleven o'clock, Zehlendorf cemetery."

"Unfortunately I won't be able to. I'm flying back to Munich tomorrow morning. Good luck with your work."

"Yes," he said, "I need it. I'm having trouble with the ending."

I saw him cross the road. He made his way slowly, walking as though he were deep in thought. The old man with the tea cozy on his head who, it now occurred to me, had probably inspired the funeral orator's example of the funeral speech made by his colleague, was still standing there, paper plate in his hand, nothing on it eaten. He was really agitated, his hands flapped and he was cursing, he cursed and spattered himself with ketchup, red-brown streaks ran down his filthy light-colored trousers, convulsive shudders ran through his body with increasing frequency.

"Hey," the man from the food stand called after me, "hey, you forgot your rose." He held it out to me.

I stopped for a moment, I thought, shall I put the rose in the trash can with the mustard-smeared paper plates. I couldn't do it. And so I walked up Kurfürsten-damm with the long-stemmed rose that hung its head in exhaustion. Some hookers were still there in their short tube skirts, one called to me: "Hey, lover boy." I walked on and wondered just why this form of address had established itself. "Hey, lover boy." Are they screw-ing up courage to make what follows more bearable for them, or are they giving their clients courage? "Come on to mama." But perhaps it's the call from far away to remember the early discoveries with one's own sex, still distinct from love, geared solely to sex. So simple, so curious. A young woman came up to me from behind a brightly lit showcase, said something to me in Polish or Russian, a sturdy woman, her thick brown hair piled high, and so young even the harsh neon light from the showcase couldn't touch her. She laughed, a cheerful open laugh that revealed a steel tooth. She held a hand out to me that I'm already about to push away when I see the note in it on which is scrawled in ballpoint:

twenty marks one trick. She pulls up the right sleeve of her blouse and I see a tattoo of two couplating dogs, the little male, sitting on top, ears flapping in wild movement, the other, the little female, under him, ears attentively pricked up and head turned devotedly to the viewer. A little work of art.

Still. I shook my head, said, "I'm here on business." She didn't understand, gestured in a touchingly helpless way toward her bosom, her heart, as if there I could find out the rest. But perhaps she wanted to let me know there was another tattoo there. I held the rose out to her and she took it and a radiant astonishment brightened her face. I walked on, waved to her once. And she waved too, called out something I didn't understand, held up the floppy rose, and laughed.

The neon advertisments glow, brand names on the ground in laser writing. The displays in the shop windows, illumined white and red, picked out by spotlights, look only more desolate for it.

There was lightning in the distance, but I heard no thunder. I decided, no matter what happened tomorrow, I'd leave. I walked along the deserted streets as if given wings by this decision to leave the city. Behind dark as well as lit windows people were copulating, others rolled sleeplessly in their beds, or read, or watched television, or got drunk, and again others waited mute and rigid. For what? The morning. An answer. An answer to what began with the Big Bang and from which no amount of reflection leads us to what might have come before or what would be after. Where are we from? Where are we going? Did it really begin with the forest retreating, the climate changing with only a few isolated trees still standing in the savannah where hyenas ran around with those powerful jaws that could effortlessly bite through an elephant's leg? And Lucy's wandering around there too. Always on her guard, she looks around, she needs to walk upright now, that way she can survey the grass, then her hands are free. I wave to her, indicate that I'm not here for any hostile reason, I only want to get to my cave, to my den which is somewhere over there.

The red tree

WHAT DREW MY ATTENTION TO THE CAR WAS the sudden glow of a cigarette inside. Walking past I saw the man sitting at the wheel, and I was certain the shadowy figure sitting in the fat, metallic night-blue BMW was the athlete in the beige suit. For a moment I wondered if I should just simply walk past, but then I thought they were sure to have my address. I'd given the phone number in the ad. And the Bulgarian had phoned me here. I unlocked the front door, didn't take the elevator but walked on the red-brown sisal runner up the stairs. A mix-up, that much must have been obvious to the Bulgarian by now. On the other hand, who asks for a taste catalogue for potatoes? If not an interested buyer, then, in their impoverished imaginations, it could only be an undercover agent or a competitor. But then it occurred to me they would have found out from a simple phone call to the hotel what I do professionally: write. And that, I thought, would definitely have alarmed them. For to these people writing means the same thing as journalism. To have someone at their heels from a news magazine frightened these people more, I decided, than the police.

I unlocked the door to the hotel—there in the hall, on the thronelike antique sofa from the 1870s with sphinxes covered in gold leaf on each side, sat Moussa. He was asleep. His head had slipped a little to one side. He was sleeping like a child sleeps. When the door behind me engaged in the lock he smacked his lips a little, perhaps in his dream he took the noise for the familiar sound of a camel chewing on its bridle. He actually smiled and slightly changed his uncomfortable position, his head slipped even further to one side. His dark-blue galabia fell about him like an artistically draped cloth.

I quietly unlocked the door to my room.

Four notes had been pushed under my door.

TIME: 7:50

Call from Mr. Bucher. Please call him. Urgent!

I stared at the note. How did Bucher know my address? I hadn't given it to him. Or had I? Had Rosenow phoned him?

TIME: 8:10

Call from Mrs. Tina. Wanted to speak to Dr. Block??? Key word: the potato in literature. Mrs. Tina

asks you—should you be Dr. Block—to call her. She
stresses: no charge!

???

TIME: 9:15

Call. Caller did not want to give name. (Man)
About potato collection?? (Caller was hard to under-
stand).
Wouldn't give his phone number. Will call again.

TIME: 9:20

Call (woman). No name. Key word taste catalogue
potatoes. Key word: comprehensive and inexpensive.
Will call again.

The hotel owner, who had seen a thing or two, must
have thought lunacy had erupted in her hotel.

For a moment I wondered whether I shouldn't just
phone the police. But to the good cop on the beat the
story would sound as if I'd dreamed it up. Should I just
lock myself in my room and wait? But then I decided it
would be better after all to go, before special units from
the Federal Crime Department blew down the door
with an open-sesame grenade. And if not the FCD,
then perhaps the beige athlete would find his way in
tonight with a skeleton key.

I drank some water from the tap, gathered up my shaving and toilet things, stuffed my shirts into my case. Wrote the hotel owner a note with the request to forward the bill but under no circumstances pass on my Munich address. And a P.S.—the one thousand and one units have been discounted. If there is still anything outstanding, put it on my bill.

I didn't take the elevator but went carefully down the stairs and out by the rear exit. The second time today that I'd used a rear exit.

I phoned Kubin from a phone booth. Considering it was after midnight I let it ring for an embarrassingly long time. I was about to hang up when Kubin answered. I asked if I could sleep at his place tonight.

"Today unfortunately," he said, "I can't do it. I've a visitor. You understand. An acquaintance, what can I say, this is her first visit. Do you have to leave your hotel?"

"They're after me."

"Who?"

"A gang of arms dealers." There was a silence at the other end of the line. I heard a faint astonished snort from Kubin, at any rate I decided the snort was astonished. "It sounds crazy, I know," I said, "I've gotten involved in a really insane business."

"Hogwash," he said. "You've boiled over with your potatoes."

"Could be that I'm mistaken," I said, "but there's also a Tuareg sitting here waiting for me."

"Where."

"Upstairs. In the hotel reception."

When I heard not just puffing at the other end of the line, but a regular groan, I said, "Listen, you know me, I've never shown even a trace of paranoia. Or have I?" Kubin kept silent. He was probably thinking it over. "I know it sounds crazy, but it's true. If you came, you'd see him sitting here, he's wearing one of those dark blue robes bleached by the Saharan sun. What's more, he's given me a ring."

"Now listen to me carefully," Kubin said in an emphatically quiet, even gentle tone. "I really can't go out now. I've been working on this evening for two months. It has to be. Today. Now. If not now, then never. You understand? So go to the drugstore, buy some valium, strength five milligrams, tell them it's an emergency, then they'll give it to you without a prescription, and then go to a hotel, a really good one, Kempinski's, for example. That's where that star Juhnke goes when he's loaded. You knock back one valium five or better maybe two, and lie down. First you phone and tell me what hotel you're in. I'll come tomorrow, first thing in the morning. Then we'll calmly talk everything over."

I laughed, it was meant to be a nice ironic laugh but sounded much too shrill, or rather, despairing. "A hotel.

Don't make me laugh. There's not a hotel room to be had in all of Berlin. People are sleeping in the corridors, in lounges. That Christo with his Reichstag wrapping has clogged up everything, without exception."

"All right," said Kubin, "I'll give you Rosenow's phone number, he always has an empty apartment somewhere."

"Thank you," I said, "but no," and hung up.

For a moment I wondered whether I shouldn't go to Spranger. I could go to him, ask him, perhaps Rogler's room was free. The heating technician who lived there was away in Brandenburg on installation work. Spranger would understand everything, after all he'd lived with the Gypsies. But then I remembered Kramer who was sure to be there and would see me with a new haircut. No. I wanted to get out of this city, fast, at once, now.

I went to the station, the last Intercity to Munich had left an hour ago. There was still a night train to Leipzig, just one train, the last before the following morning, a milk tain, a riffraff collector that stopped at every station, laid on specially for the Christo business. I still had a little time, still half an hour.

I went to the waiting room to buy a cola. A man was pushing an electric machine that sandblasted trodden chewing gum off the freshly-laid granite. A crackling squeaking noise that almost blotted out a song in the distance. I walked off following the direction of the song. Outside stood the rejected, the despairing, those laden with tribulation, filthy, stinking of schnapps and piss, men and women, old and young, they stood there and listened. A man was singing. A Russian. He was singing Russian and German songs. He sang in a wonderful, deep bass, so melodious and with such volume that I feared for the panoramic window in front of which he was standing. He sang and at the same time held a hand to his right ear as if he were listening to his own singing. He sang:

> Thoughts are free, who can guess them?
>   Like night's shadows they flee,
>   no one can know them,
>   nor hunt them with powder and shot;
>   thoughts are free!

And then I realized what Red Tree meant: an inn. It was the name of an inn!

> And if in a dark cell they lock me,
>   they do it in vain:
>   For my thoughts, they tear
>   barriers down and tumble walls:
>   for thoughts are free!

I went over to the man and put a ten-mark note in his cap.

He bent down and collected the money from the hat. Picked up a shabby cardboard suitcase battered at the corners, said: "Now I can go. My good sir, I wish you, your parents if they are still alive, and if you have a wife, your wife, your children, and, if you have a lover, her too, health and happiness."

"Thank you," I said.

"Are you leaving tonight?"

"Yes."

"If you will permit me the question, where are you traveling?"

"Leipzig."

"Oh," he said, "how convenient. I want to go there too and with your money I've enough for the fare." He showed me a hand full of silver coins. The cuff of his sleeve was worn through, the loose threads neatly cut off, but you could still see the fiber of a cheap shiny material. "You would be doing me a great favor if we could walk together."

"Why?"

"The station police here are rather intrusive."

I went with him to the ticket window. He bought a ticket. I stood and waited. Two policemen did in fact approach, one leading a Doberman with a wire muzzle. The three came toward us, their eyes fixed on my companion. He pocketed the ticket and said: "So, now we can be on our way," and laid his hand on my arm in a friendly gesture. The two policemen sized me up for an instant, then pulled away the Doberman that had picked up my scent, and went on their way.

"These dogs don't like Chanel, strange, of all perfumes the one Marilyn Monroe is supposed to have worn at night. It affects the animal's sense of smell. You don't need a lot, a trace is enough. I get these small sample bottles from the perfumery," said the man.

I went with him up the steps to the track where the train was waiting, one of those run-down, fast milk trains that stink of shit. "Do you smoke," he asked.

"Yes."

"If it wouldn't disturb you, we could sit in the same compartment."

I didn't dare say I had a first-class ticket. I sat down with him in one of those smoke-filled compartments with the socialist plastic seats that, in this heat, make your trousers stick to your buttocks.

"Where would you like to sit?"

"It's all the same to me."

"If you don't mind, I'll sit by the window."

I sat down by the door diagonally opposite.

The train started. Outside the lights of the street lamps and illuminated windows slipped by.

He offered me a cigarette, a dark, almost black Russian brand. "Really I shouldn't," he said, "because of my voice. Oh well."

I said, "Thank you, I'd rather smoke a cigar." I took out my tortoiseshell case and held it out to him: "Please help yourself."

"But there are only two left," he said.

"Yes," I said, "when they're smoked I'll quit. Then I'll have finished my work."

"What work, if you don't mind me asking?"

"I wanted to write a story."

He took the cigar carefully and gingerly, sniffed it, "Thank you. Wonderful. At the Last Judgment I shall throw this cigar onto the scales for you."

"It will weigh very little," I said.

"Sometimes a feather can tip the scales."

He gave me a light. "If you don't mind I would like to turn out the light," he said.

"Go ahead."

He switched off the light. Only a faint emergency light was still on above the door. "You're less disturbed this way," he said. Outside the lights slipped by. He smoked, and in the semi-darkness I saw that he was a connoisseur. He smoked and his face beamed the way I remembered my uncle when he—which happened extremely rarely—smoked a good cigar.

The conductor came, checked the tickets, sniffed and said: "A good brand!"

"Cohiba Exquisito," said the man opposite me, showing himself to be a true connoisseur. In this dim lighting he could have been a businessman, or perhaps, in that old-fashioned jacket with its too-wide lapels, more likely a collector of contemporary art accompanied by a gallery owner with a rather strident haircut.

In the half-light the worn, frayed cuffs of his jacket didn't show.

"Have a good journey," said the conductor.

"Thank you. It's friendly of you to sit in a compartment with me."

"One can't sleep here anyway," I said, "and at least we can talk. You know Cohiba?"

"In the old days, on rare occasions, we also had them in Moscow. Courtesy of the socialist brother. Connections. Under the counter. Only to be had through good connections."

"You speak very good German."

"Thank you. I was a singer at the opera in Sverdlovsk. Before that I studied German and Italian, and a year here in the former GDR."

"How long have you been in Berlin?"

"Almost two months. But the controls on immigrants have gotten worse over the last few days. My passport isn't of the best quality. And then I'm not allowed to sing anymore where I used to sing, in the Fehrbelliner Platz subway."

"The police?"

"No, my compatriots. They hand out licenses. But I was working free-lance. It's not advisable to quarrel with the Chanel faction."

"Who are they?"

"Well, our Russian friends." He smoked, looked

closely at the cigar wrapper: "Didn't you, how can I put it, yourself make a precipitous exit from the city?"

"Yes, you could put it that way."

For a moment the train came to a halt where work was being done on the line, harsh floodlights, the metallic screech of a milling cutter. Machinery, a massive crane truck, workmen wearing yellow coveralls with reflector belts, sound of pickaxes, another metallic screech. Then the train slowly moved forward again.

"Do you know what Red Tree means?"

"No."

"I had an uncle who could taste the varieties of potatoes. And then when he was dying he said Red Tree. My mother was amazed, everybody wondered what it could mean. At first I thought it was a kind of potato. As he was a great potato connoisseur. And just now when you were singing I remembered what it meant. It was the name of an inn. The Red Tree. A story he'd told me, I must have been seven or eight at the time. I'd remembered the story but forgotten the name of the inn until just now. It didn't seem important. He was my favorite uncle. He could never say no. And he was considered lazy. He spent a great deal of time sitting or lying on the sofa. Smoked, told stories that weren't very exciting. He had a lot of time for me. He simply couldn't say no. His father must have been very different. He was an agricultural worker. In Meck-

lenburg, on an estate. He must have been a very stub-
born man, the exact opposite of this uncle. One day,
this would have been just after the turn of the century, a
social democratic agitator came to the district to recruit
for the Agricultural Workers Union. And there was to
be a meeting at an inn. No one was supposed to go, the
estate inspector had forbidden all the workers. No one
went, only my uncle's father, he took the boy, who was
eleven or twelve at the time, with him. On the way they
met the estate inspector in his dogcart. He said, if you
go, you're fired and instantly, is that clear?

"No, said the father and went on his way with the
boy. The two of them sat in the room at the back at the
inn, a man and a boy. There was nobody else. The agitator spoke. The inn, as I said, was called The Red Tree.
Nothing political. It referred to a frontier barrier. Between Mecklenburg and Prussia. Red Tree meant a
frontier. And it was one my uncle's father had crossed.
So political as well after all. After the social democrat's
speech the father returned with his son, my uncle.

"And that same night they had to pack their things
and leave the farmhands' quarters. And so they moved
out at night, with one of those wooden cannon carts,
their few possessions, blankets on top, the other farm
laborers and maids, inside, behind bolted shutters sang:
Thoughts are free."

He drew calmly on the cigar, laid his head back, and

slowly from the depths the smoke came wafting out of his mouth as he spoke.

"Where did they go?"

"They moved around. They had a rough time. My uncle's father was considered a rabble-rouser, word soon got around. So for months they lived only on the potatoes they secretly dug up in the fields. The strange thing is my uncle didn't get sick of this, instead, as a child, he always paid attention to the differences, he learned to appreciate the minute variations in taste. All his life he liked potatoes. That's how I remember him: eating fried or mashed potatoes, and then he could tell you what kind they were. That's why he was often invited in the bad old days, as a potato connoisseur, as it were. And he'd sit on the sofa and smoke. He could blow three smoke rings, one through the other, that's something I've never seen since."

"How did he do that?"

I blew a ring that wasn't bad, the second was a bit shaky, hurried after the first, the third was nothing but a little cloud.

The Russian first took a deep breath, then again, drew on the cigar, laid his head back as if he wanted to drink the smoke, just like my uncle. And then sent one, two smoke rings out into the compartment—proper rings, and then, after a long pause came another ring, small, wonderfully compact, and round.

"I'll be damned," I said, "fantastic!"

"It's a question of the breath," he said, "you have to breathe correctly as you do when singing, not simply pump your chest full at the top, but breathe in deeply into your diaphragm, you need to feel it here." He un-buttoned his jacket. I saw that he was wearing suspenders and that his trousers were much too wide for him. He pointed to his lower ribs and then took a deep breath so that he actually broadened under them. Then he exhaled three times, slowly but forcefully. "This way you have a greater volume of air and you can expel the air with more control. Try it." I did and he watched me. "Very good," he said. "Try again."

I did it again, without smoking, the cigar in my hand. Inhaling so deeply and then forcing the air out made me a little giddy.

"Now, with the air under your diaphragm, smoke, draw in the smoke with your last inhalation, it won't reach your lungs, it'll stay in your mouth, and then you'll easily blow out three rings. All you then need do is find the right rhythm, that's to say breathe out at the right moment, then it's a matter of practice or just plain luck. You'll see if you try this a few times, it's the secret of a really good cigar, you'll feel a real euphoria. Like with witches' sabbath. That's the nightshade family. Above all, don't tense up, the same lightness in smoking as when you breathe."

We sat there for a moment, in that racket from the rails, smoked and said nothing. Outside it was dark. Just once a few lights flitted by.

"May I ask," he said, "why you're so pleased to get away from the city tonight?"

"Strictly speaking, this story begins with my not being able to find a beginning. I sat at my desk and pondered, I roamed through the city. I took up smoking again, cigars, hoping that, swathed in smoke, the right, the absolutely essential beginning to a story would occur to me."

I breathed in deeply, once, twice, and then one more time drew hard on the cigar and blew out the first ring, slowly and calmly, not at all with the intention of blowing out three. It flew out small, round, and compact, slowly turned into a large circle, I'd already sent out a second smaller ring hurrying after the first and now really did have enough breath for a third, the smallest, which I blew out forcefully, yes, with all my strength, feeling slightly dizzy, and knowing that I was about to succeed at this moment in something I'd probably never manage to do again. And then!—then the small ring effortlessly caught up with the second, flying through the medium one just as it pushed through the big one; and the little one, then the medium, and last the big one, all three were moving away in reverse order; slowly and already slightly unraveled they flew into the semi-darkness where they dissolved slowly into a fine blue haze.

Author's note

After having been separated into two countries for over forty years, Germany was reunited in 1990. Not only had the German-German border divided two countries, it had also separated two societies as well as their respective economic systems. Following the collapse of the socialistic German Democratic Republic (GDR) state enterprises were privatized, i.e. were sold to the private sector by means of a specially instituted state agency. The name of this agency was "Treuhand" (True hand). As could be suspected, transactions and sales were not always dealt with in the most truthful manner.

This division of Germany into an eastern socialist GDR and a western capitalistic Federal Republic of Germany (FRG) was especially poignant within the capital city of Berlin. The city had been divided for a good thirty years by a wall. East Berlin was the former Russian zone, and West Berlin had consisted of the American, British, and French zones. The fall of the wall in 1990 did not, however, lead to the subsequent disappearance of the wall within the German mentality. Critical differences between the bearings and culture of eastern and western Berlin have endured to the present day, between the "Ossies" (East) and the "Wessies"

(West). These differences reach into the very language of the city, into the Berlin dialect.

Dialects in Germany are often the colloquial languages and are significantly older than the Standard German that encompasses them. The Bavarian dialect in southern Germany, for example, is often depicted as rural and circumspect. With numerous assimilated words from Yiddish and French, the Berlin dialect in northern Germany is often described as quick, sharp-witted, slick, and street wise. The Berlin dialect is, in fact, spoken more quickly than the majority of other dialects. Interestingly enough, it is spoken far more deliberately and articulately in the East than in the West. These are all minute, yet audible differences that accentuate the contrasts between the eastern and western cultures determined by German history.

This history, a history which has been so calamitous for the world, was aesthetically thematized by means of an artistic venture on the part of Christo and his wife Jeanne-Claude. In June 1995 the artists veiled the German Reichstag, the parliamentary building erected at the turn of the century, with synthetic canvas. This colossal undertaking drew hundreds upon thousands of curious visitors to Berlin.

At present Berlin is an immense construction site. From an ideological and architectural perspective it is a chaotic city, vibrant and bustling with an aggressive, yet creative atmosphere. This is one reason why I have pitched camp in this city for the time being and, like an ethnologist, am pursuing field work for a new novel which will also be set in Berlin.

December 1997   UWE TIMM